Duchessina

A YOUNG ROYALS BOOK

Duchessina

A Novel of
CATHERINE DE' MEDICI

Carolyn Meyer

HARCOURT, INC.

Orlando   Austin   New York   San Diego   Toronto   London

Requests for permission to make copies of any part of the work
should be submitted online at www.harcourt.com/contact or mailed
to the following address: Permissions Department, Harcourt, Inc.,
6277 Sea Harbor Drive, Orlando, Florida 32887-6777.

www.HarcourtBooks.com

Library of Congress Cataloging-in-Publication Data
Meyer, Carolyn, 1935–
Duchessina: a novel of Catherine de' Medici/Carolyn Meyer.
p. cm.
Summary: While her tyrannical family is out of favor in Italy, young
Catherine de' Medici is raised in convents, then in 1533, when she is
fourteen, her uncle, Pope Clement VII, arranges for her marriage to
Prince Henri of France, who is destined to become king.
1. Catherine de Médicis, Queen, consort of Henry II, King of France,
1519–1589—Childhood and youth—Juvenile fiction.   2. Italy—
History—16th century—Juvenile fiction.   [1. Catherine de Médicis,
Queen, consort of Henry II, King of France, 1519–1589—Childhood
and youth—Fiction.   2. Kings, queens, rulers, etc.—Fiction.
3. Convents—Fiction.   4. Orphans—Fiction.   5. Clement VII,
Pope, 1478–1534—Fiction.   6. Italy—History—16th century—
Fiction.]   I. Title.
PZ7.M5685Duc   2007
[Fic]—dc22   2006028876
ISBN 978-0-15-205588-2

Text set in Requiem Text
Designed by Lydia D'moch

First edition
A C E G H F D B

Printed in the United States of America

Duchessina is a work of fiction based on historical figures and events.
Some details have been altered to enhance the story.

For Ramona,
and in memory of George

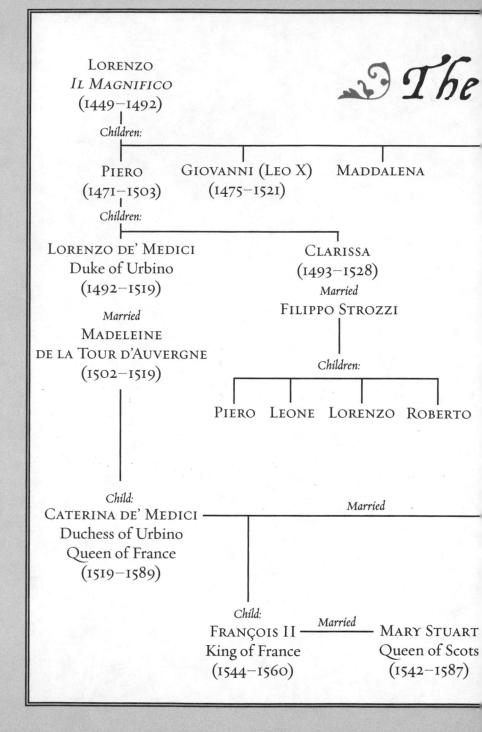

LORENZO
IL MAGNIFICO
(1449–1492)

Children:

PIERO
(1471–1503)

GIOVANNI (LEO X)
(1475–1521)

MADDALENA

Children:

LORENZO DE' MEDICI
Duke of Urbino
(1492–1519)

Married
MADELEINE
DE LA TOUR D'AUVERGNE
(1502–1519)

CLARISSA
(1493–1528)

Married
FILIPPO STROZZI

Children:

PIERO   LEONE   LORENZO   ROBERTO

Child:
CATERINA DE' MEDICI ——————— *Married*
Duchess of Urbino
Queen of France
(1519–1589)

Child:
FRANÇOIS II —— *Married* —— MARY STUART
King of France   Queen of Scots
(1544–1560)   (1542–1587)

The

Medici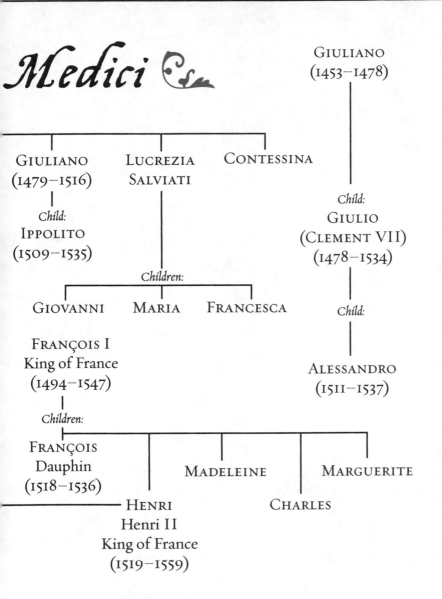

GIULIANO
(1453–1478)

GIULIANO
(1479–1516)

LUCREZIA
SALVIATI

CONTESSINA

Child:
IPPOLITO
(1509–1535)

Child:
GIULIO
(CLEMENT VII)
(1478–1534)

Children:
GIOVANNI   MARIA   FRANCESCA

Child:

FRANÇOIS I
King of France
(1494–1547)

ALESSANDRO
(1511–1537)

Children:

FRANÇOIS
Dauphin
(1518–1536)

MADELEINE

MARGUERITE

HENRI
Henri II
King of France
(1519–1559)

CHARLES

Duchessina

1

Beginnings

"YOU ARE A MEDICI," Aunt Clarissa used to tell me. "And you are destined for greatness. Never forget that."

And I have not forgotten, even though my very existence has been threatened—not once or twice, but many times. Before I was a month old, both my mother and my father were dead. Yet I have survived and endured. Not everyone is pleased about that. At my christening I was named Caterina Maria Romula di Lorenzo de' Medici. When I was a child, those who loved me called me *Duchessina*—Little Duchess. Now my enemies have begun to call me *Madame Serpent*. No doubt they have their reasons.

This, then, is my story—and how my destiny was fulfilled.

———

THE ENORMOUS Palazzo Medici—a ground floor and two upper floors—was an entire world, entered from the street through a grand arched portal and a foyer leading to a large inner courtyard. Marble statues stood silent guard among splashing fountains. I spent the days of my early childhood with my nurse, Elisabetta—I called her Betta—in a suite of rooms overlooking the courtyard. Sometimes I watched from my window as important visitors arrived, handed their horses over to the grooms, and climbed the broad stone stairway to the *piano nobile,* the main floor of the palace where Cardinal Giulio de' Medici received them in his vast apartment.

From Betta I learned part of my story:

"You came into this world at eleven o'clock on a Wednesday morning, the thirteenth of April in 1519. Three days later your aunt Clarissa and I carried you to the Medici family church of San Lorenzo for your baptism. Our hearts were bursting with grief as well as hope, for your mother had fallen victim to childbed fever and your father had been ill for some time. Less than two weeks later your mother's bright soul left her suffering body. In another six days your father's soul went to join hers."

I wept when my nurse reached this point in my story. How unfair it seemed that death had snatched my parents from me before I had a chance to know them! I cried for them, but mostly I cried for my orphaned self.

As I grew, I became curious about other parts of the palace. When I thought I could escape Betta's watchful eye, I began to explore. Betta had a habit of falling asleep over her needlework every afternoon following our mid-day dinner. I was supposed to be resting, too, but as soon as Betta nodded off, I crept down the narrow stairway from my apartment to the main courtyard. Beyond that I found a second, more interesting courtyard, where servants hurried back and forth and the business of the palace was conducted. Through a small door leading to a dark and scary passageway I could get to the splendid gardens, alive with bright flowers and trees and birds and sparkling fountains.

During these explorations, I made a surprising discovery: Two boys, much older than I, shared a large apartment on the top floor with their servants and tutors. I hid from the boys, slipping behind the thick columns or squatting in one of the shadowed doorways, and listened to their conversations. The older boy, who I learned was called Ippolito, was handsome, polite to the servants, and good-natured, always ready to laugh. The younger boy, Alessandro, appeared to be just the opposite: He had a cruel mouth, frizzy reddish hair, and a dark scowl. He spoke rudely to the servants, mocked his tutors, and haughtily argued with Ippolito. I disliked this Alessandro and wanted Ippolito for a friend, without ever having spoken a word to either of them or even knowing exactly who they were. I thought the boys were my secret, and I didn't mention them to Aunt Clarissa or Betta.

One day when I was not quite four, I crouched quietly

in the main courtyard. No one paid me much attention. I was intently observing a small lizard as it skittered across the smooth paving stones when the two boys thundered noisily down the stairs from their apartment. Alessandro spotted the little lizard at once and lunged at it. I had tried a few times to catch it, or one like it, but it was always too quick for me. I had decided it was better simply to watch it. Now Alessandro had it in his ugly paws, and in an instant he had pinched off its tail.

Ippolito, my friend who didn't yet know that he was my friend, protested. "Don't be cruel," he told Alessandro sharply, but Alessandro merely laughed at him.

"It'll grow a new one," Alessandro said, heartlessly poking his victim.

Could it really grow a new tail? I wondered. I didn't know, but I felt deep sympathy for the poor lizard. Unable to keep still any longer, I popped up out of my hiding place. "And what if it does not?" I demanded, glowering at Alessandro.

He jumped back, startled. "Well, well!" he cried. "What's this?"

"It's *la duchessina!*" said Ippolito, smiling at me. I couldn't resist smiling back.

"Such tenderness you show for small creatures," Alessandro said with a smirk, dropping the tailless lizard. It tried to scurry away, but Alessandro put a speedy halt to that. He stomped on it, ending its short life and leaving a bloody mess on the stones.

"You killed it!" I cried, horrified. "How could you *do* that?"

Alessandro glanced at me with heavy eyelids lowered disdainfully, looking somewhat like a lizard himself. "Perhaps you'd like to offer a prayer for the deceased? Or maybe we can ask His Eminence the cardinal to say a mass for it."

I burst into tears and ran away, the sound of Alessandro's harsh laughter grating in my ears.

Ippolito ran after me. "Duchessina, wait!" he called. Obediently I stopped and allowed him to take my hand. "May I call you that? We should get to know one another. We're cousins, you know. Like you, we are under the direction of our uncle, Cardinal Giulio. His good friend, Cardinal Passerini, is our principal tutor. I'm sorry you witnessed such cruelty. I make no apologies for Alessandro—that's simply the way he is, and I've made up my mind that I must tolerate it, since we're always together. Can we be friends, then, you and I?"

I gazed up at the handsome boy who offered me friendship. He bent down and kissed the hand he still held. "Friends?" he asked again, arching one dark eyebrow.

"Friends," I agreed. But I was still troubled by what I had just witnessed. "Is that nasty boy your brother?" I asked, thinking they did not resemble each other in any way.

"No, no—Alessandro is a cousin, also. We live in a world of uncles and cousins, and no one is exactly who he says he is."

I wanted Ippolito to stay and tell me more about who he was and where he'd come from and who the dreadful Alessandro was and where he fit into this puzzle. But Ippolito simply smiled again and strode off in search of his despicable companion.

THOUGH I LIVED at Palazzo Medici under the guardianship of Cardinal Giulio, it was the frequent visits from Aunt Clarissa, my father's sister, that I looked forward to. When she thought I was old enough to understand, she told me more about who I was.

"You are descended from an ancient family," Clarissa said proudly. "The Medici is a family of great prestige and enormous wealth. They amassed a fortune through trade, in spices from the East and cloth from Europe, and an even greater fortune in banking. There is no greater family in Florence or in all of Tuscany—indeed, in the whole of the Italian peninsula."

She told me about my great-grandfather, the first Lorenzo de' Medici, known as *Il Magnifico*—the Magnificent. He had reigned like a prince over the city of Florence. The Medici coat of arms appeared everywhere. One of *Il Magnifico*'s sons became Pope Leo. "He was the first pope from Florence," Clarissa said. "The city went mad with joy when he was chosen."

But the Medici also attracted jealousy and hatred. The people had once enjoyed *Il Magnifico*'s rule, but the mood changed. They wanted to rule themselves. Even during my great-grandfather's lifetime there had been attempts to drive the Medici from power. "As the daughter of Lorenzo, Duke of Urbino, you are the last of the Medici line descended from *Il Magnifico*. You need to understand all this, dear Caterina, for your own good. Life may not always be easy for you."

She told me that from the beginning it had not been easy for me. Within a few months of my birth, I had contracted a terrible fever.

"You hung suspended between life and death," my aunt remembered. "We prayed over you night and day, and thanks be to God, you survived. I wanted to take you into my home and bring you up as my own dear child, but your uncle, Pope Leo, ordered you brought to Rome. I dared to argue with him: What did he know about raising a girl? But he would not relent. I begged to be allowed to accompany you. This time, Pope Leo agreed, and off we went to Rome with Betta and a large retinue."

"And our uncle? How did His Holiness receive me?" I asked eagerly. Her answer always heartened me.

"The Holy Father unwrapped your fine linen swaddling, looked you over from the top of your curly head down to your sturdy little feet, and pronounced you fine and fat. Then he sent me back to Florence, saying he had no further need of me. You would stay in Rome, in the care of his sister, Lucrezia Salviati. I could hardly bear to leave you."

I had no memory of any of it, except that I did seem to

recall a fat, jowly man with sparkling gems on his fingers. While I was still an infant, Pope Leo gave me my father's title, creating me Duchess of Urbino. That was when everyone—everyone but Aunt Clarissa—began to call me *Duchessina.* To my aunt I always remained Caterina.

I had been in Rome for two years when Leo suddenly sickened and died, a victim of Roman fever, caused by the bad air of the swamps surrounding the city. When Leo had first become pope, he'd brought his cousin, Giulio, to Rome as his chief assistant and made him a cardinal. After Leo's death, Cardinal Giulio decided to return to Florence and to take me with him to live at Palazzo Medici. Although he was only a distant cousin of Pope Leo, Giulio insisted on calling himself my "uncle."

"You can't imagine how happy I was to have you back in Florence," Aunt Clarissa said. "Now I could visit you nearly every day."

ONCE A MONTH Cardinal Giulio called for me to be brought to him for a kind of inspection. These visits always unnerved Betta. If the cardinal found any fault with me, it was sure to be a reflection on her care. I knew she was nervous, because she always tugged at the snarls in my hair with more impatience than usual. Hair combed, faces and hands washed, clothes neat, we made our way through a series of connecting rooms that were hung with tapestries, until we were announced at the cardinal's most private studio. Cardinal Giulio didn't smile or rise to greet us but stayed seated behind his writing table.

"She remains quite small," the cardinal said, peering down at me and pursing his thin lips. "Does she eat well?"

Betta dutifully recounted dishes I had eaten recently. My uncle frowned and urged that I be fed more meat, especially veal, as well as macaroni. "But not too much fresh fruit. It's known to be unhealthful for children," he said. "Allow only dried figs, *per favore.*"

Betta promised to do her best, although I made her task more difficult by pleading for fresh figs, which I loved, as well as cherries and pears.

Sometimes Aunt Clarissa came from nearby Palazzo Strozzi, where she lived with her husband, Filippo, and their children, to accompany me on visits to the cardinal. Our uncle would question her about the development of my manners. "Progressing nicely," my aunt would assure him, and to prove her right, I would execute a dainty curtsy, moving my left foot back and bending my knees as I had been taught.

My greatest fault, though, was my inability to remember to keep my eyes modestly lowered. I was always gazing around curiously or unflinchingly meeting the looks of whoever was inspecting me. I had not yet learned how to steal sidelong glances.

"Why don't you ask *me,* Your Excellency?" I asked. "I would gladly answer your questions." Speaking out too boldly when questioned was another fault.

Cardinal Giulio's eyes bored through me. "The child still has much to learn, Clarissa," he said, his lips drawn in a disapproving scowl.

I committed yet another error by staring back at him frankly and then made matters worse by asking, "Exactly what do you want me to learn, Excellency?"

"To quell your impertinence," snapped the cardinal. "Now leave us."

WHEN I TURNED FOUR, I gained more freedom to roam around the palazzo, and I learned more about my cousins, our "uncle," and this palace in which we lived our mostly separate lives. Ippolito was fourteen, and Alessandro nearly twelve. Naturally, they had little in common with a four-year-old girl. Almost every day I saw the boys' principal tutor, Cardinal Passerini, hurrying somewhere with an imperious air, shouting orders to the servants. I knew the servants didn't like him; I saw the faces they made when he wasn't looking. Except for the dreaded inspections, Cardinal Giulio remained a remote figure whom I saw only on feast days when he celebrated Mass at San Lorenzo.

I was not yet considered old enough to eat at the table in the palace dining room or to join the festive dinners served in the beautiful garden. Instead, I took most of my meals in my apartment with only Betta for company. Occasionally, though, I was allowed to attend special feast-day dinners. Cardinal Giulio de' Medici sat at the head of the table, his shrewd glance darting around the crowd, but my attention remained fixed on Ippolito and Alessandro.

Betta claimed to know little about the boys. "You must ask Signora Strozzi," she said. "Your aunt can tell you more than I can."

"Who are those boys?" I asked Aunt Clarissa when she next came to visit. I was already digging into the packet of sweets she'd brought, little jellies flavored with saffron and formed into animal shapes.

"Your cousins," she answered vaguely. "Through the kindness of our uncle the cardinal you've all been provided a home here and an education and a good life."

I recognized this as the kind of thing adults said when they didn't want to explain things to children. And, anyway, I already knew that much. "But who are their parents?" I persisted.

"You wouldn't know them," she said, and briskly changed the subject. "Have I told you that the seamstress is coming to make you a pretty new gown for the Feast of Corpus Domini? I was thinking that pale blue over yellow silk would be lovely. Don't you agree, Caterina?"

FOR A WHILE I stopped asking questions about Alessandro and Ippolito. But lonely little girls have a habit of hovering in places they are not supposed to be and listening to the gossip of servants who have forgotten about the child perching quietly on a sack of grain in a shadowy corner of the pantry, pretending to play with a doll.

One day I was wandering through the kitchen where a dozen cooks and helpers were plucking fowl, boning fish, stirring soups, rolling out dough for ravioli and lasagne, all in preparation for the Feast of Corpus Domini. Everyone was too busy to pay any attention to me. Suddenly, amid the rattle of pans and clash of knives, an angry cry went up. Alessandro raced by, making off with two ripe melons and a pile of almond cakes. The baker ran after him, shaking his fist.

"Lorenzo's bastard," the baker muttered when he returned red faced and empty-handed. "*Il Moro* is worse than worthless, and a thief in the bargain."

Lorenzo's bastard? Lorenzo, my father—was he Alessandro's father, too? My aunt had never mentioned that. How could such a despicable boy be my father's son? It couldn't be! I would not believe it! It had to be a different Lorenzo.

But the very possibility made me ill, so ill that shortly after that scene in the kitchen I was put to bed with a fever and a bad stomach. For two days I refused to eat. Each time I fell into a restless sleep, I woke up sobbing. Betta sent for Aunt Clarissa, who hurried to see for herself what ailed me. I finally confessed to her the cause of my illness.

"The wicked Alessandro is my brother!" I cried. "I would rather die than have it be true!"

"Who told you such a thing?" Clarissa demanded.

"I heard the servants talking," I said, not wanting to

cause trouble for the baker. "They called him 'Lorenzo's bastard.'"

"Don't believe slanderous gossip," she advised me. "It's hardly ever true. And what were you doing in the kitchen?"

"Nothing," I said, which was not quite the truth—I'd been looking for fresh figs and cherries. "But why do they call him *Il Moro,* the Moor?"

I watched anxiously as Aunt Clarissa paced the room, her chin cupped in her hand. Finally she stopped and gazed down at me. "Listen, Caterina, I'll tell you whatever you wish to know about your cousins if you will first promise to drink some veal broth and then to sleep until the bell rings for vespers."

I promised to do as she asked.

My aunt sat beside me on my great bed. "Alessandro is a bastard, it's true. But your father isn't Alessandro's father, so you may rest easy about that. Alessandro is the son of a cardinal, and his mother was a Moorish slave—that's why they call him *Il Moro.* No one is permitted to speak of Alessandro's relationship to the cardinal, although almost everyone suspects it. Because your father, Lorenzo, is dead, it's easier to pretend that *he* was the boy's father."

Alessandro, the son of a cardinal? My aunt had not mentioned the cardinal's name, but I thought I could guess: loudmouthed Passerini. This new information was nearly as shocking as what I'd overheard in the kitchen. But I felt greatly relieved. At least the ruffian Alessandro was not my brother.

"And Ippolito?" I asked. "What about *him*?"

"That's not a secret. He's the son of Pope Leo's younger brother, Giuliano, who drowned when Ippolito was just a boy. Leo was very fond of the child."

"And his mother?"

Aunt Clarissa merely shrugged. "Ippolito's a bastard, too."

ONLY A FEW months after my fourth birthday, a far-off event altered the course of my life. Pope Leo's successor died after only a year in office—poison was suspected—and Cardinal Giulio rushed off to Rome, determined to get himself elected as the next pope. The household gathered to watch my uncle's departure from Florence in a splendid procession. I wasn't at all saddened. His heart, I felt, was cold and dry and had no room in it for me.

When the news was relayed back to Florence that Cardinal Giulio de' Medici had indeed been elected, the city rejoiced. He took the name Pope Clement VII and placed his good friend, blustering Cardinal Passerini, in charge of the Palazzo Medici and of my two cousins and me.

Now that he was pope, Clement instructed Passerini that he wished to have me live in the most splendid manner possible. I was given several new gowns and hooded cloaks, more servants to dress my hair and wait on me, a richly carved bed and thick mattress stuffed with wool, and a much grander apartment to make room for all of this. Naturally, I found all of these changes exciting.

"But why?" I asked—my favorite question.

"The Holy Father wants to show you off like a precious jewel," Betta said, "to make you a more desirable marriage prospect when the time comes."

"I have no need of marriage prospects," I confided. "I'm going to marry Ippolito. But don't tell anyone. I don't want Alessandro to know."

Betta rolled her eyes. "I won't breathe a word of it," she promised.

IT SEEMED THAT Pope Clement was not the first to think about marriage prospects for me. When I mentioned it to Aunt Clarissa, she told me another story, beginning with the marriage of my parents.

"It came about like this," she said. "Pope Leo decided to send his nephew, Lorenzo de' Medici, to the christening of the firstborn son of the king of France. Leo had already chosen a bride for Lorenzo: Madeleine de la Tour d'Auvergne, a cousin of the French king. Lorenzo was as handsome as Madeleine was beautiful. The moment they met, Madeleine fell madly in love with Lorenzo, and he with her. She was just sixteen. He was twenty-six. Three days later they were married."

I savored every detail of their wedding: my father in a fur-trimmed doublet, my mother in a gown of aquamarine silk embroidered with pearls, her hair caught up in a garland of jeweled threads. As vivid in my mind as though it were a painting by Raphael, this was the sole memory I had of my parents.

"You were born a year after their wedding," Clarissa continued. "And then we lost them both. When Pope Leo insisted that I leave you in Rome, I was terribly worried, for I had no idea what was going to happen to you. Because your mother was French-born, King François sent his ambassador to take you to live at his court. But you had inherited not only your mother's vast fortune but also your father's, and Leo was not about to hand the richest girl in the land over to the French! He'd begun to think of a suitable husband for you before you even cut your first tooth. He ordered a pretty little *cassone* to be made for you by the most talented wood-carver in Rome."

I still had that *cassone,* a small wooden chest, richly carved and painted, in which I kept my two most precious possessions—my mother's ruby cross and my father's gold ring with the Medici seal.

Aunt Clarissa went on with the story. "Leo told me, 'When she's wed, we'll see that she has a much larger one. Several of them! And we'll fill them with the finest silks, the most opulent jewels a Medici bride has ever owned.' So this is nothing new, Caterina. The subject will come up again and again, until Pope Clement finds you the best husband in the world."

2

Palazzo Medici

ONCE I HAD PASSED my fifth birthday, Cardinal Passerini assigned a tall, gaunt lay brother named Fra Matteo to be my tutor.

"I've never been a teacher," Fra Matteo confessed on the first day we sat down together at a table in the cardinal's library. "Do you know how to read, Duchessina?"

"No," I said. "Do you?"

His pale face colored a bit. "*Sì,*" he said. He pulled a thick book from the shelves. I recognized the Holy Scriptures. "We may as well begin at the beginning." He began to read aloud in Latin: *In principio creavit Deus celum et terram.* "In the beginning, God created heaven and earth."

I followed his finger as he traced the marks on the page, but I didn't understand a thing. Then he explained about letters and words, and after a while I began to see how it all fit together. I was learning to read.

After I had been studying with Fra Matteo for several months, I asked him about a drawing that hung on a wall of the library. "What's that a picture of?" I asked.

"It's a map," explained my tutor. "If you were an angel high up in heaven looking down on the earth, that's how it would appear to you." With his long, bony finger he outlined the shape of a boot. "This is the Italian peninsula, and that's the sea almost surrounding it."

He pointed out the location of Tuscany and Florence where we lived, and Rome where the pope lived, and the duchy of Urbino, from which my father had taken his title and I now took mine.

The map fascinated me. Every time I went to the cardinal's library for another lesson, I studied that map. One day I asked Fra Matteo what lay beyond its edges. He unrolled a map of Europe and showed me England and France and Spain. I gazed at it for a long time.

"My mother was from France," I explained, and the sight of my mother's country so moved me that I came close to weeping. "Someday I'll go there."

"Perhaps you shall," said Fra Matteo, rolling up the map and directing my attention back to my studies.

NEXT TO BETTA and Aunt Clarissa, my favorite person was Ippolito. I liked him immensely and watched for him,

hoping to find him alone so that I could have his attention and his kind smiles all to myself. Such moments were
rare. But my feelings about horrid Alessandro only became worse as time passed. I wasn't the only one who
avoided him. His nasty tongue and outbursts of temper
kept everyone at a distance. I wondered how anyone
could be so ill-humored.

I seldom left the palazzo, usually only to venture the
few steps to the parish church of San Lorenzo in the company of several ladies—wealthy friends of Cardinal
Passerini—and two Tartar slaves. The ladies, all heavily
jeweled and veiled, generally ignored me, but their disinterest didn't bother me, for I wasn't much interested in
them. I rarely saw children of my own age, except when my
little journeys took me as far as Palazzo Strozzi, even
larger and grander than our palazzo, to visit my aunt
Clarissa and her husband Filippo and their four sons, my
real cousins. When Passerini discovered how much I
looked forward to these visits, he used them as a reward,
meted out for good behavior, withheld when I displeased
him. This angered me and taught me to deceive when
necessary and admit to nothing.

My eldest Strozzi cousin, Piero, a serious boy, much
like his father, was four years older than I. The next,
Leone, sweet tempered but not terribly bright, was just a
year older. Lighthearted Lorenzo was younger, and
Roberto was an infant still living in the home of a wet
nurse in the country to be cared for until he was weaned.

Once her duty to produce several Strozzi sons had been fulfilled, Clarissa declared her longing for a girl.

"I've always wanted a daughter," she told me. "Every night I pray to the Holy Mother that I may be blessed with one—or, better yet, more than one! Naturally, though, my husband is pleased, as any banker would be, that sons don't require dowries in order to marry well." She leaned close and hugged me. "But I do believe, Caterina, that a gracious God has sent you to soothe my heart that aches so for a little girl!"

If I'd been allowed, I would have gone in an instant to live with my aunt and her family. I sometimes dreamed of that. But such a thing was clearly impossible for a child to ask for—I didn't even think to mention my yearning to Passerini. I had to learn to be content within my small, restricted world: my sumptuous suite of rooms, with occasional escapes to the courtyard, the kitchen, the garden, and the chapel.

The kitchen was where I watched the bustling activity and listened to the raucous chatter of the cooks and bakers who prepared the two big meals served each day, the first at midday and another in early evening. In the courtyard I observed the comings and goings of high-ranking visitors to Cardinal Passerini, although why anyone would want to spend time with him I could not imagine. In the garden I enjoyed the birds and flowers and the small creatures that made their home there. But the place I came to know and to love most dearly was the Chapel of the Magi.

The small, windowless chamber was lighted only by flickering candles. On each wall a painting on plaster showed a part of the procession led by the magi, wise men from the East, on their way to Bethlehem to worship the infant Jesus.

The men wore fine garments richly embroidered and bejeweled. Their horses pranced through green wooded hills, and birds soared across an azure sky. Horses, dogs, deer, cattle, sheep, even camels and a cheetah, crowded the frescoes that covered three walls of the chapel. Candlelight reflected on the gilded crowns and the silver tips of lances.

The artist had portrayed everyone in the procession, even the three wise men, as citizens of Florence, many of them prominent members of the Medici family. Aunt Clarissa identified some of them. A handsome boy with blond curls and blue eyes, dressed in white brocade, rode a high-stepping white charger. Aunt Clarissa insisted that the boy, representing the youngest of the wise men, was supposedly *Il Magnifico.*

"He looks nothing like the portraits I remember from my childhood," she mused. "But that's who everyone says he is."

The procession followed that golden-haired boy, whoever he was. How I would have liked to have *him* as my friend!

The Chapel of the Magi became for me a secret treasure—a chamber where I could lose myself in the fantastical scenes and imagine myself as a part of them.

Princes, churchmen, shepherds, citizens, slaves—but nowhere in the entire procession could I find a single grown woman, or a young maiden, or a little girl like me. Maybe they had all been left behind in the large white castle at the top of the hill in the distance, watching the procession from one of the narrow windows. And so I gave myself a place in the midst of the procession—nothing too large or prominent, just a small figure off to one side, riding behind the golden-haired boy. I half closed my eyes and dreamed that I was there, dressed in silks and velvet and pearls, mounted on a fine white horse—Caterina de' Medici, *la duchessina,* on her way to worship the Christ child!

One day as I was lost in my fantastic dream, the door of the chapel flew open, and a short, wiry man with a crown of wild, uncombed hair loomed in the doorway. I shrank myself as small as I could in one of the carved wooden choir seats, hoping to escape notice. But the chapel was not large, and he quickly spotted me.

"Ha! I've caught a little mouse!" he boomed in a voice that seemed too big for his small size. "Come here, little mouse."

Frightened, I sat perfectly still, as though made of stone.

"Well, then," he said, "at least tell me: What do you think of all of this?" He waved his arms at the frescoes.

"I very much admire them," I admitted cautiously.

"Oh, you admire them, do you? And what would you say, little mouse, if I told you the whole lot isn't worth a fig? Pretty pictures, that's all they amount to. Scarcely even art, let alone *great* art."

"I'd say that you are wrong, because I'm quite fond of them," I said. Still a little frightened, I went a bold step further: "And I would like to be a part of them."

The strange man examined me more closely, and I in turned examined *him*—his bushy, untrimmed beard; eyes that burned with intensity; a misshapen nose; a high fore-head furrowed with lines like a plowed field; an unsmiling mouth. "Tell me, little mouse, do you have a name?"

"I am Duchessina. And do *you* have a name, *signore*?"

"Michelangelo Buonarroti, at your service," he said with a formal bow. "I am a great artist—the greatest in the world," he added. "I have painted the ceiling of the Sistine Chapel in Rome. I have sculpted the *Pietà* in St. Peter's Basilica. And perhaps *la duchessina* has seen the sculpture of David that stands in the Piazza dei Signoria?"

I shook my head.

"No, I suppose not. A statue of a nude male is not suit-able viewing for a little mouse." He smiled mirthlessly, ex-posing darkened teeth. I wondered if he was half mad, but he no longer scared me—I sensed that he meant me no harm. After a while the strange artist began muttering to himself, seeming to have forgotten that I was there. Even-tually he turned and left, still muttering, "Must find that devil Passerini," and I was alone again with my beloved pictures of the magi.

———

DAY AFTER DAY I watched glumly as my two older cousins made their presence felt—one loudly and boorishly, the other gaily and pleasantly—around the palazzo. They were often in the company of Cardinal Passerini or one of their other tutors. Sometimes I saw them dressed to go out in their bright-colored clothes, stockings trimmed with silver lace, Alessandro in a pink cape, Ippolito in his blue satin tunic. They wore jaunty feathers in their velvet caps and golden chains around their necks and carried scented gloves, and they were off to roam the streets of Florence, out of sight of the cardinal. Sometimes I heard them returning toward dawn, singing loudly, laughing at nothing.

Being a girl and so much younger, I was naturally excluded from their activities. When the two were together, they shunned me. This was better than having Alessandro notice me. Michelangelo was right, I thought: better to be a little mouse, quiet in my corner, seeing everything without being seen.

But sometimes I was unlucky. Surly Alessandro pounced, delighted when he managed to make me shriek. I trained myself not to give him the pleasure of reacting. *I will not jump when he startles me,* I vowed. *I will not weep when he says something cruel.* And I promised myself that I would never run to Cardinal Passerini or my aunt or Betta, carrying tales about what dreadful thing Alessandro had said or done to me. It took immense self-will not to cry, but I gradually gained mastery over my feelings.

Then one day he sneaked up behind me and shouted, "Frog!"

I spun around and glared at him. "Why do you call me 'frog'?" I asked, more calmly than I felt.

"Because you look just like one. Those popping eyes of yours—they're like a frog's," he said with intolerable smugness. "Have you seen yourself in a mirror? If you have, then you know what an ugly little thing you are." Alessandro smirked and strolled off, leaving me standing there, too stunned and hurt to reply, tears pricking my eyes in spite of my vow.

Is it true? Am I ugly?

I was about six years old then, and until that time I had never considered whether I was or was not beautiful. No one had spoken of it. There were no little girls in the palazzo with whom to compare myself. But there were a great many serving girls and kitchen helpers and chambermaids, and I had noticed that those with small waists, generous bosoms, delicate skin, abundant hair, and winsome smiles were the ones who seemed to have the easiest time of it, to beguile the men in order to get their way.

Michelangelo, the artist—the genius—had called me "little mouse," and I hadn't minded. But on that day, with that one cruel remark, Alessandro planted a seed in my heart. I understood that I was not beautiful, as a woman should be, and that I would have to find clever ways to get what I wanted.

———

ON A SPRING DAY just before my seventh birthday, Cardinal Passerini left Palazzo Medici with Alessandro to spend time at one of his hunting lodges. Ippolito, who was suffering from a catarrh and didn't feel well enough to accompany them, stayed behind. After he had mostly recovered and his cough was improved, Ippolito surprised me in the palace garden. I was sitting in a pergola and practicing on the lute. I had a good ear for music and had learned to play well enough to accompany myself while I sang.

"I thought I heard an angel," he said. "And indeed I did!"

I smiled. Much nicer to be called "angel" than "frog"! Or even "mouse."

He begged me to continue playing while he sat quietly nearby, nodding his approval. Lilac and lavender bloomed all around us, perfuming the air. Sometimes Ippolito sang with the tunes he knew, despite a hoarse voice. This scene was repeated over several days, to my great pleasure.

Then Alessandro and the cardinal returned from their hunting trip, both of them bragging about the number of deer they had managed to kill, and the idyll ended.

But I did not forget it.

ONE LONELY DAY followed on the heels of the next. A year passed with little to disturb my routine. As a young child I didn't understand the political strife that set the rulers of Europe at each other's throats, but I soon grasped that conflicts among kings and emperors and popes could drastically affect my life. Fra Matteo explained it.

In the year that I was born, Charles V, the king of Spain, had been elected Holy Roman Emperor, a title that gave him power over much of Europe. Emperor Charles and King François of France hated each other and waged war against each other until, in one final battle, Charles took François prisoner, finally agreeing to release him in exchange for the French king's two sons. For four years he kept the two little boys as hostages in a Spanish prison. Pope Clement had been an ally of King François. But now, with François soundly defeated, Emperor Charles held the fate of the pope, the city of Florence, and all of the Medici clenched in his powerful fist.

During the spring of 1527, as I was about to turn eight years old, disturbing rumors began to drift into Florence. Fra Matteo told me that Charles had ordered twenty thousand soldiers to march south to Rome. Each time we heard a new rumor, I quietly visited the cardinal's library and studied the maps my tutor had taught me how to read.

"The emperor intends to show Pope Clement who's in charge," Fra Matteo speculated when these rumors turned out to be true. "He's determined to teach the pope a lesson."

The rumors became much more frightening. The emperor's soldiers were storming through Rome, murdering, raping, and pillaging as they went. No one wanted to believe the awful stories. There was no word from Pope Clement.

When Aunt Clarissa and Filippo heard the tales brought by traders from as far away as Naples and picked up by the Strozzis' servants in the market, my aunt rushed to our palazzo, accompanied by her Ethiopian slave, Minna. I was supposed to be at my lessons, but even my tutor, whose family was from Rome, found it hard to think of anything but what was happening there and what might happen next in Florence.

"What a catastrophe!" Clarissa cried, slumping onto a bench, her fingers buried in her hair. "I will not try to deceive you, Caterina," she told me. "I'm very uneasy about the future. Trouble will surely come to this city as well. Filippo's banker friends say that feeling against the Medici is mounting steadily here, as it has in the past. We must prepare ourselves."

"For what?" I asked tearfully as my dull but safe little world shook and seemed about to crumble. "What can we do?"

"Don't worry," she said, jumping to her feet. "I'll think of something."

And since I had no one else, I had to trust that she would.

FOR SEVERAL DAYS we had no further news from Rome. Hardly anyone slept. Meals were cooked and served but left mostly untouched. Then one night the uneasy silence was shattered by a furious pounding on the main portal, the clatter of horses' hooves in the courtyard, and persistent shouting.

I flew from my bed, but Betta seized me by both arms. "Stay where you are, Duchessina," she insisted. "Do you hear me? I'll go down to find out what's happening."

I pretended to obey, but headstrong as usual, I followed her.

Torches flared in the courtyard. Two weary travelers—a young cleric and an older priest who had agreed to undertake the dangerous journey—were calling for Cardinal Passerini. When the cardinal at last appeared in his scarlet robe and hat, the priests delivered to him a letter from Pope Clement. Members of the household gathered while Passerini read the brief letter, his fat cheeks and small eyes grotesque in the flickering light.

His glance swept over us, all waiting silently—cooks, grooms, gardeners, laundresses, valets, and maidservants, as well as Alessandro and Ippolito and their gentlemen dressed in silks and velvets. I crept close to Betta and hung on to her hand, sticky with sweat.

"The emperor's soldiers are bent on destroying the Eternal City," the cardinal announced gravely. "But— thanks be to God—our great friend, His Holiness Pope Clement VII, is safe. He sends his assurances that we in Florence have nothing to fear." Passerini forced a ghastly smile and waved his hands as though he were shooing us away. "Now, I beg all of you, return to your beds for a good and peaceful night's rest, knowing that, with God's grace, all will be well."

No one moved. "Tell us what it's like there, *padre*," the cook called out to the young cleric. "You've seen it. Tell us."

"No questions," the cardinal interrupted, his voice like the screech of metal on metal.

"On a cloudy night as mist rose from the swamps and shrouded Rome," the younger man said softly, ignoring the cardinal, "the maddened soldiers broke through the ancient walls of the city. They rampaged through the streets like wolves, looting homes of rich and poor alike, desecrating churches, raping nuns and pious housewives, slaughtering everyone in their path. The waters of the Tiber ran red with the blood of bodies dumped there."

Betta clapped her hands over my ears to shut out the gruesome images, but I shook her off.

The older priest took up the story in a breaking voice. "The invaders destroyed our ancient monuments and treasures. Wherever they found books, they burned them. If they discovered precious manuscripts, they tore them to shreds. They stabled their horses in the Sistine Chapel beneath Michelangelo's glorious ceiling."

We listened without wanting to hear but were powerless to stop ourselves. Even Cardinal Passerini could not bring himself to turn away.

"When Pope Clement realized what was happening," the young cleric said, "he fled through a secret passageway."

This last bit of news struck the household like a lightning bolt. Cardinal Passerini's cruel mouth stretched in a grimace. "Lies! Slander!" he cried in a high, thin voice. "The Holy Father does not run from difficulties."

The priests lapsed into silence, drained of emotion. Only then did most people begin to shuffle out of the courtyard, shaking their heads, unable to speak.

3

Flight

BETTA HALF DRAGGED me toward the stairs. I hung back, peering over my shoulder, and observed the glances and whispered words exchanged between Passerini and my two cousins. *What is he telling them?* I wondered, stumbling along after Betta.

Soon the palazzo was quiet again, although I doubt that anyone was asleep—except Betta, who had resumed her throttled snoring. Wide awake, I crept from my bed, pulled a dress over my sleeping shift, and stole silently out of my bedroom.

This wasn't the first time I had left my apartment in the darkness of the midnight hours. Relying on the map in my head, I made my way from room to room, counting seventeen paces to the first door, twenty-two to the second, careful to avoid the large oak table; six more paces to the left brought me to the top of the stairs. Then I counted each stone step to the landing and continued on down until I arrived in the empty courtyard. Smoky torches in iron brackets threw shuddering splashes of light among long, shifting shadows.

Clinging close to the walls, I crept by the night guards dozing near the main portal. I moved through the shadows toward the second courtyard, hoping to overhear the conversations of sleepless servants. But as I passed the entrance to the passageway leading down to the stables, I saw that the door stood ajar. Curious, I peeked in, expecting to see the grooms tending to the exhausted horses ridden by the two priests from Rome. Instead, I saw three fresh horses saddled and ready for their riders: Cardinal Passerini's sorrel mount, Ippolito's gray stallion, and Alessandro's bay. *Are they leaving? What's going on?*

Hearing voices, I slipped behind the door and out of sight. Ippolito rushed in, dressed for traveling, a long cloak over his tunic and a leather bag slung over his shoulder. I was too surprised to remain still. "Ippolito, where are you going?" I asked, stepping out of the shadows.

Startled, he swung around, dropping the leather bag. "Duchessina! What are you doing here? *Per favore,* go back to your apartment before the others come. The cardinal won't be pleased to find you."

"Not until you tell me where you're going. And I don't give a fig if the cardinal isn't pleased!"

Ippolito looked exasperated, but he took both my hands in his and spoke gently. "We must flee—Alessandro and I. Hatred of the Medici is growing by the hour. Passerini is afraid there will be an uprising, and the rabble will come after us. The cardinal is taking us away to his palazzo in Cortona, to wait until things are calmer here."

"I, too, am a Medici," I reminded him. "Surely I am in danger as much as you!" Suddenly I was angry at this cousin, whom I had adored until I saw him preparing to flee to safety, leaving me behind. *And more Medici than you,* I thought. In my anger I came close to saying the words that must not be said: that I was a true-born duchess and he was only a bastard. But I swallowed those words and said instead, "Why can't I go with you?" My lip was trembling, partly from fear, partly from fury.

Ippolito laughed, and I hated him for that. Then he knelt down, still holding my hands. "Dear little cousin," he said, looking into my eyes. I felt myself weakening, the anger draining away, replaced by hurt. "It will be a long, hard ride, and you would be very unhappy, I'm certain. But don't worry—your aunt Clarissa will care for you," Ippolito assured me. "You can depend on her. Soon we'll all be together again, and everything will work out for the best. You'll see, Duchessina!"

His brilliant smile brought back a rush of my feelings for him, and I wished that his horrible cousin and the dreadful Passerini would never come back.

Ippolito tenderly kissed my hand. "The others will arrive here at any moment," he said, rising, "and they will be very angry to find you here. *Per favore,* Duchessina, go back to your bed and sleep well. I'm certain that our aunt will come for you tomorrow and make sure that you're out of harm's way and happy as well."

"Couldn't Aunt Clarissa see to your safety also?" I asked.

Ippolito shook his head. I would have continued protesting, but I heard low voices in the courtyard and recognized Alessandro's sarcastic tone.

"Go now, Duchessina! At once!" Ippolito whispered urgently, and hurried to fasten the leather bag to the saddle of his horse.

I quickly hid myself behind a manger and watched resentfully as the three prepared to leave. A short time later Alessandro, Ippolito, and Passerini led their horses up the ramp from the stables and out through a side door. The hooves of the horses clattered on the paving stones. When the sound had faded away, I rushed back up to my room and flung myself, sobbing, onto my pillow.

I MUST HAVE slept a little, for the sun was already high when I heard shouting in the street and excited voices in the courtyard.

Betta hauled me out of bed, babbling, "Mistress, it's happening, the people have gone mad! A mob is forming at the gates!"

We dressed hurriedly and ran down to the courtyard, where there was much confusion. "Where's the cardinal?" the servants were shouting. "Has anyone seen him? He needs to speak to those at the gates. He must do something—but where is he?"

Their panic increased my own. Didn't they know yet that Cardinal Passerini had deserted us, left us to fend for ourselves?

The side door opened, the same door by which Passerini and my cousins had left, and Aunt Clarissa stepped in, followed by Minna, her slave, who slammed the door and bolted it. Immediately Clarissa measured the situation: There was no one in charge. "Where's Passerini?" she demanded.

I flung myself into her arms. "He's gone," I whispered.

"Gone? Gone where?"

"Cortona." I told her what I had seen in the stables a few hours earlier.

"Accursed coward, that Passerini!" she spat. "I'm not surprised. All right, we must act. No one will do it for us."

Seizing the arm of the nearest manservant, a groom from the stables, Aunt Clarissa ordered him to carry a bench to the center of the courtyard and then to help her climb on it. "Stay close to me, Caterina," she ordered, though I didn't need to be persuaded.

"Now listen to me, all of you," Clarissa cried, her clear voice ringing in every corner of the courtyard. "Our beloved cardinal has departed, in order to save his own skin," she said, her words dripping with scorn. "The young gentlemen, Ippolito and Alessandro, have accompanied him. Many of you may wish to follow their example, and you are free to do so. Others may choose to stay, and to you I entrust the care and protection of Palazzo Medici, which has been your home. It is my duty to see to the well-being of my niece, *la duchessina*. I intend to secure her safety, and then to return here as soon as I'm able. Have any of you anything to say?"

For a moment the crowd in the courtyard was silent, except for the shuffling of feet. Then the cook spoke up. "God go with you, mistress," he boomed. "And with *la duchessina*. I for one intend to remain here, with my wife and children. We're loyal to the Medici. They've been good to us."

The cook's fat wife and four stout daughters gathered around him. A few others—the head gardener, several kitchen helpers, and two of the grooms—moved to stand with him. But as we watched, several people edged toward the door; others wavered, heads down, eyes lowered. Outside the palazzo, the shouting grew louder and angrier, sending chills down my back.

"Mille grazie," Clarissa said simply. "A thousand thanks." She stepped down from the bench.

A guard, ashen faced, made his way to her side. "Signora, they're demanding to see the cardinal. I told them he's not here, and that made them even angrier. A few are beginning to call for *la duchessina*." He glanced at me and quickly looked away. "They want her brought out to them."

"Hold them off as long as you can. If you must, tell them she'll come out soon." Then Clarissa turned to a groom who had pledged his loyalty. "We'll need a cart and a donkey," she told him. "Throw some straw in it and a few sacks of grain. A little dung, too, but not too much. Do you understand me?"

The groom bowed. *"Sì, signora."*

Clarissa led me up the stairs to my apartment. I obeyed, not daring to question her. Betta followed, wringing her hands. "Signora Strozzi," she said in a breaking voice, "where are you going?"

"To Poggio a Caiano," my aunt replied, mentioning the Medici villa in the hills outside of Florence. "Caterina should be safe enough there."

"She may be safe once she's there," Betta said. "But the journey out of the city won't be safe for either of you unless you're disguised." Betta suddenly became calm and businesslike. "Allow me to find you both suitable clothing and to accompany you. I'm sure you'll find me very useful."

The furor beyond the palazzo walls was growing more intense. Fists pounded on the main portal. I shivered and fought back a sob. "All right," Clarissa agreed. "Hurry."

"Am I to come as well, *signora*?" asked Minna.

My aunt opened her mouth to reply, but Betta interrupted. "There is no way that country folk would have a black slave," Betta bluntly told my aunt. "And no way I can disguise her."

Clarissa thought a moment. "You must return to Palazzo Strozzi," she instructed. "And tell Signor Strozzi I've gone to Poggio a Caiano with *la duchessina*. Assure him that I'll return as soon as it's safe."

Betta helped my aunt exchange her fine clothing for one of Betta's plain smocks. If I hadn't been so frightened, I might have laughed at her transformation from noble lady to peasant woman. Betta disappeared to the servants' quarters while Clarissa packed a canvas bag with her silk gown and a few items for me. I clutched the little *cassone* in which I kept my mother's ruby cross and my father's gold ring.

My nurse reappeared, bringing a boy's tunic, trunk hose, and well-worn cloth cap. "You'll travel as a boy," Betta said. "They won't be looking for a boy."

With my hair pinned up under the cap, I was no longer recognizable as *la duchessina*, and I was so pleased with the disguise that I felt less afraid. The three of us hurried down to the stables. The groom had harnessed a donkey to a cart used for hauling everything from refuse headed for the dump to live pigs destined for the spit. I wrinkled my nose from the smell. I saw my aunt swallow hard. Betta, unperturbed, announced that she would drive the donkey.

Clarissa and I climbed into the cart and allowed the groom to pack baskets and sacks around us and buried the *cassone* deep in the straw. The groom flung open the door to the street and spoke up loudly enough for anyone around to hear.

"Get on with you now," he said gruffly, "and don't be wasting any time or I'll make sure the master hears about it!"

"Ah, shut your mouth!" Betta retorted.

I was shocked to hear them speaking so rudely to each other, until I realized this was part of the disguise. Betta slapped the reins on the donkey's back, and we started off.

But not quickly enough. Several members of the mob saw the donkey cart and surrounded it. "Where do you think you're going, old hag?" one of the men shouted, his red face shoved close to Betta's.

Betta hurled back an insult, and I raised my fist and made a gesture that I had seen the servant boys make when they didn't know I was present. I had no notion what it meant, but the red-faced man did. He bellowed something, spit flying from his lips. Betta goaded the donkey into a brisk trot. Soon we were free of the rabble and rattling toward the city gates. Only two young guards stood duty at the tower. They caught a whiff of our rank load and waved us through without bothering to ask any questions. The odor was enough to put an end to their inquiry.

Once outside the walls of Florence, we settled down for the ride through rows of tall black cypress and into the rolling hills. The sun flooded the olive groves and vineyards with a golden glow. At the first farm we reached, Betta flagged down a young peasant boy, not much older than I was, and offered him a few coins to unload the disgusting dung and garbage that was steaming in the hot sun. While he shoveled, we settled in the shade of a large tree by the side of the road, and the boy's mother brought us wine and bread and some meat and cheese. We ate hungrily—never had a meal tasted better. Aunt Clarissa declared her nerves calm once more, and she kissed Betta at least a dozen times for her cleverness in disguising us and getting us away from the angry mob.

"Now we're safe," she said.

While we ate and rested, traffic flowed along the road to Pistoia, a market town that lay some distance beyond Poggio a Caiano. Most people were on foot or rode donkeys or drove farm carts similar to ours. But as we were finishing the last of our meal, a company of soldiers rushed by, the brass buttons of their uniforms flashing and the flanks of their horses gleaming in the noonday sun. Betta and Clarissa idly speculated where the men might be headed.

We clambered back into the cart, the filthy load now replaced with fresh, sweet-smelling straw, and continued on our way. Soon our donkey cart rolled into the village of Poggio a Caiano. Past the piazza the road climbed steeply toward the walls of an ancient fortress. At the crest of the hill stood the villa that *Il Magnifico* had built behind the old stone walls. Betta drove the donkey cart toward the main gate, flanked by a pair of guard towers. As we approached, soldiers poured from the towers and blocked our way.

"Those are the soldiers who passed us on the road," I said.

"But what are they doing here?" Clarissa wondered aloud. "I didn't tell anyone but Minna that we were coming."

Someone from the palazzo, I thought; *maybe somebody bribed a servant, or threatened him—or her.* I was frightened again, and sweat began to trickle from under my cap.

"It's probably nothing," Betta said, flicking the reins and urging the donkey to move on.

An officer stepped forward. "Identify yourselves," he barked.

"Just some poor country folks, come to deliver grain to the master's house," Betta called out in the cringing voice I'd often heard servants use when they had to grovel before their master. *Are they always putting on an act?* I wondered.

The captain ordered one of his men to inspect the sacks of grain. I wished now that we hadn't paid the farm boy to clean out the dung and filthy straw; that might have put off the inquisitive soldier. The captain was staring at me. I glanced nervously at the spot where the canvas bag with my *cassone* was buried in the straw. "You, boy," he said, stepping closer and addressing me. "What's your name?"

We hadn't prepared for this moment. I opened my mouth, but nothing came out. "He's dumb," Betta answered for me. "Can't speak a word. Born that way, poor lad." Holding her thumb to one nostril, Betta blew her nose. Snot landed at the captain's feet. He grimaced and stepped back.

"Get on, then," he said. "But what can you be thinking to enter through the front gate? Go around to the back."

And so we did. But our problems weren't over yet. Clarissa had to find the steward in charge of the villa, convince him of our identity, and persuade him to let us in—and quickly.

We were greeted by an elderly groundskeeper who had been awakened from his siesta by our arrival. His white hair was uncombed, his buttons done up wrong, and his mood grumpy. "And who might you be?" he asked gruffly. He didn't recognize us in our disguises.

"This is *la duchessina*," Clarissa informed him, lifting off my cap and allowing my long, dark hair to tumble onto my shoulders. Then she opened the *cassone* and showed him the Medici ring. "She has escaped an angry mob in the city, and she needs a safe haven here. Who are those soldiers? What do they want?"

The groundskeeper jabbed his thumb in my direction. "Her," he said.

Clarissa sank onto a bench and ran her fingers through her hair, a familiar gesture. "Come sit by me, Caterina," she said tiredly, patting the place beside her. "I must decide what to do about our situation. We can't remain in disguise for long—we'll soon be found out. I'll go to speak to the captain and see what can be done."

Later, after the steward in charge of the villa had welcomed us properly and Clarissa had changed out of Betta's smock and looked once more like the imposing lady that she was, she kissed my forehead and strode boldly out to the guard tower. I watched from the loggia.

I couldn't hear what my aunt said to the captain, but I could see from her gestures that she was enraged. She came storming back to the villa, her face streaked with tears. Angrily she wiped them away.

"The new governors of Florence are furious that Alessandro and Ippolito have gotten away from them. They're determined to have you as their hostage, to make sure they get what they want, and Captain Rinuccini, the officer in charge, has been ordered to make sure that you don't slip through their fingers again."

Hostage! What was going to happen to me? I was almost too frightened to hear what she said next.

"Tomorrow they will take you back to Florence, to the Santa Lucia convent in the Via San Gallo. And there you will stay, no one can say for how long. I tried to convince the captain that you'd be better off at another convent— Santa Lucia is known to be unsympathetic to the Medici family—but he has his orders from the governors. I can't prevent it from happening. The nuns may not like you, but I believe you will be safe there. Captain Rinuccini has sworn that as an oath."

You said I would be safe here, I thought, my feelings a confused whirl. "What about you, dear aunt?" I sobbed.

"I'll take my chances with the rest of Florence," she said, her dark eyes flashing—whether with anger or tears, I couldn't say.

"But when will I see you?" I asked fearfully.

"Dear child, only God knows that. But I will think of

you every moment and pray for you night and day until we're together again."

We collapsed into each other's arms and wept until we had no tears left. That night I scarcely slept, although Betta did her best to soothe me with the songs she often sang when I had trouble falling asleep.

The next morning Captain Rinuccini and the soldiers came for me. I clung to Aunt Clarissa, too scared to move. Betta hovered nearby, wringing her hands and muttering.

"Be brave, Caterina," Clarissa whispered. "No matter what they say to you, remember who you are—a Medici!"

After more kisses and sad farewells, the captain lost patience and snatched me up. He set me on a great white horse, led by a soldier in a bright uniform with shining buttons. Clarissa thrust my *cassone* into the captain's hands. "See that no harm comes to her," she half ordered, half begged.

Just eight years old, I rode back to Florence to meet my fate, whatever it was.

4

Santa Lucia

The separation from Aunt Clarissa, and from Betta, too, was so wrenching that even now I can scarcely bear to think about it. Surrounded by soldiers, I passed the farm where only the day before we had stopped to rest on our way to Poggio a Caiano. The boy who had cleaned out our cart and the old woman who had given us bread and cheese and wine stopped their work to stare as the company rushed by on the road to Florence. The boy and I exchanged glances, but he could not have known that the girl in the velvet cloak was the same person as the boy in the cap he had met the day before.

The sun blazed overhead when the soldiers escorted me into the walled city through a western gate within sight of the majestic red dome of the cathedral. We rode

by peasants selling eggs, chickens, early fruits, and vegetables brought from their farms in the countryside. We
passed the church of San Lorenzo and Palazzo Medici. I
gazed up at the windows, searching for a familiar face,
someone who might help me, but the palace looked deserted, the Medici coat of arms smashed. A small crowd
gathered in Via San Gallo, gaping, and watched us pass.
The soldiers closed ranks around me, but a few people
must have recognized me. An old woman ran toward us,
waving her bony arms and shouting, "Down with the
Medici!" and the soldiers pushed her away so roughly that
she fell, still making angry gestures. Others picked up her
cry, *Down with the Medici!* The soldiers drove back the
crowd, and we hurried on.

We halted before the ironclad wooden doors of the
convent of Santa Lucia. I didn't want to be there, but I
saw there was no way to escape. At least, I thought, I
would not have to endure the shouted insults. Captain
Rinuccini unceremoniously swung me off the horse, set
me on my feet, and handed me my *cassone*. A small door
within the great doors creaked open, and the captain exchanged a few words with a shadowy figure on the other
side. A pale hand reached out and dragged me inside, and
the small door slammed shut. "Wait!" I shouted after the
captain, suddenly in a panic. "Don't leave me here!" But
the captain was gone.

I found myself in a barren courtyard without a plant or
a tree or even a niche in the wall for a statue of the Blessed

Virgin. A pudding-faced nun glared at me, meaty hands planted on her hips. "So you're Caterina de' Medici," she said. *"La duchessina."* Her voice was as gruff as a man's.

Clutching the *cassone* so hard that the corners dug into my flesh, I tried not to cry, but tears welled in my eyes. I brushed them away. All I could do was nod.

"Speak up, girl!"

"Sì," I managed to whisper.

"'*Sì, Suora Madre*'!" she said sharply.

"Sì, Suora Madre," I repeated. The tears spilled over.

The mother superior turned and walked swiftly toward a dark corridor. I hung back, not sure what I was supposed to do. When she realized I wasn't following her, the mother superior stopped and spun around. "Why are you standing there like an ox?" she demanded. "Come this way."

I hurried after her, up two flights of steep stone stairs and through a succession of gloomy rooms until we reached a door that opened into a small, dark chamber. "You'll stay here," she said.

The cell contained only a wooden stool and a low bed covered by a coarse blanket; a crudely carved crucifix hung above it. Dampness stained the cracked plaster walls, and a little light leaked through a small, dirty window near the ceiling. It smelled of must, of poverty and neglect. Somewhere a bell tolled.

"Get rid of that gown and cloak and put on that tunic—it's all you'll be permitted here," said the mother superior, pointing to a shapeless garment hanging from a peg. "Then come to the chapel. The bell has rung for sext." She hesitated. "Understand, Caterina de' Medici, that you are here by order of the governors," she said. "The Medici are hated here. Nothing pleases us more than their fall from power." The mother superior stalked off, slamming the cell door behind her.

No one, not even the awful Alessandro, had ever spoken to me so harshly. I flung myself on the narrow bed, weeping. Aunt Clarissa's advice came back to me: *No matter what they say to you, remember who you are—a Medici!* But what good did it do to remember that now, in this place where we were hated?

"I hate you, too," I sobbed.

When I'd run out of tears, I sat up. The thin mattress was stuffed with straw. I was used to sleeping on mattresses filled with soft wool and covered with fine linen sheets. I rubbed the rough cloth of the tunic between my fingers. I had worn only smooth silks and velvets all of my life, and I didn't like the feel of this. I took off my familiar clothes and pulled the tunic over my linen shift. It was ill fitting and as ugly as a grain sack. I wrapped the *cassone* in my gown and cloak and stuffed the bundle under the bed.

Where was the chapel? I stepped out of the cell and listened until I picked up the distant chant of women's voices. Following the thread of sound, I arrived at a cloister, a covered walkway surrounding a small open square. There were no growing things. No birds sang. A few heavy drops of rain began to fall, splattering onto the broken tiles. At first I thought the cloister was deserted. It was as though nothing could live in this place. But something *did* live here: A large rat ran over my feet and skittered across the open space. A chill crawled down my spine, and I leaped up, smothering a scream.

The chanting grew louder as I ran from the cloister. It led me to a bleak chapel where dozens of nuns knelt in rows on the dusty stone floor. A few glanced up furtively as I entered, but none met my eye or moved aside to make room for me. I found a place near the back and knelt. The nun beside me turned and looked directly at me with dark eyes set too close together above a large beak of a nose that reminded me of a hawk's. She stared at me for a moment and then edged sideways—whether to allow me more space or to get away from me, I couldn't say.

The chanting of a psalm began: *Those who act deceitfully shall not dwell in my house,* intoned the nuns on the far side of the chapel, and the nuns nearby responded, *and those who tell lies shall not continue in my sight.* The far side continued, *I will soon destroy all the wicked in the land,* and the others replied, *that I may root out all evildoers from the city of the Lord.*

The hawk's eyes bored into me as she repeated those words: *that I may root out all evildoers.* Her look was so spiteful that I wanted to jump up and flee from the chapel, from the convent itself. Even if I managed to find my way out, where could I go? If I ventured onto the streets, I would likely be captured and harmed. But if I stayed here, surely I would not be killed, even if the nuns hated my family.

I fixed my gaze on the painting of the Blessed Virgin and tried to frame a prayer that would convince her to get me out of this place. I prayed that Aunt Clarissa would come for me, or my cousin Ippolito, or Betta, or Pope Clement, *anyone*! I prayed that I would not be left here and forgotten.

NOT KNOWING what to do or where to go when the prayers had ended, I returned to the cloister and sat on a low wall, keeping an eye out for the rat. The rough tunic chafed my skin. Before I'd left the villa in Poggio that morning, I had been too upset to eat more than a little bread with pork jelly, and now I was hungry. My empty stomach ached and rumbled. I sat and waited, wiping away the tears that rolled down my cheeks. Now and then one of the nuns hurried by, skirts swishing. No one spoke to me.

I knew a little about the way the convent day was divided into hours for prayer, for work, and for meals and sleep. Later, at the ringing of the bell when the nuns returned to the chapel to chant midafternoon prayers and psalms, I again knelt beside the hawkeyed nun. She seemed to expect me. I wanted to ask her how I could get some food, but I was afraid. And so I waited.

At last, after the late afternoon prayers, when I thought I would faint from hunger, I followed the nuns to the refectory, a large chamber where they took their places on crude benches at long, bare wooden tables. Lay sisters carried in bowls of stew, gristly meat floating in a salty broth, and slabs of coarse, dry bread. The pudding-faced mother superior blessed the dismal food, which was then eaten in silence. I hungrily choked it down, remembering the dinners prepared by the cooks at Palazzo Medici: juicy roasted meats and boiled fowl, spicy fish pies, baked pastas with lots of cheese, fresh vegetables and fruits, delicious cakes and custards. The memory was a torment.

Still not knowing where to go or what to do when we were dismissed at the end of the meal, I returned again to the cloister. I think I would have welcomed the rat for company. Instead, the hawkeyed nun came to sit on the wall near me. She told me that her name was Suor Immacolata.

"And you are Caterina de' Medici, Duchess of Urbino," she said, languidly drawing out the syllables. "Daughter of Lorenzo de' Medici, Duke of Urbino," she continued. "Am I correct? I knew him well." She imitated a smile.

"You knew my father?" I asked, too eagerly. I should have guessed from her false smile that no good would come from this conversation.

"Oh, indeed I did. I knew a great deal about Lorenzo de' Medici. What would you like to know about him, Duchessina? He was handsome—no denying that," Suor Immacolata said bitterly. "Nor can it be denied that he was lazy and arrogant, selfish and spoiled—and none too bright in the bargain. Or that I was a servant in his father's household, the daughter of the steward in the service of his father. Lorenzo ruined me—as he did many of the young virgins in his family's employ—and left me to bear his child. A little girl like you, Duchessina! I left her at a convent when she was only two days old. Imagine that! Somewhere in Florence is your half sister, serving rich girls whose fathers send them to be educated by the nuns until they're let out to marry a rich man."

I was no match for this resentful woman. I should have gotten up and walked away from her, refused to listen to her tale, but it was as though millstones were attached to my feet. I could barely bring myself to form any words that would stop her mouth. "You speak ill of the dead," I finally managed to whisper.

She laughed hollowly. "And I suppose you believe that his death was a tragedy! Well, perhaps so, for you. But I can tell you, your father lived a life of dissipation and debauchery. It was the French disease that took his life—not consumption, as I'm sure you've been told."

"French disease?" I asked innocently.

"It wasn't only naive servant girls whom Lorenzo bedded," she informed me, pouring her poison into my ear. "But prostitutes as well. They infected him with their filth. It couldn't have been a pleasant way to die. A wonder he didn't make me a gift of the pox as well as of a daughter."

I somehow shook myself free of the paralyzing fear that had nailed me in place. "No more!" I cried. "No more!" And I ran blindly away, back to my cell. Her words echoed in my head: *Somewhere in Florence is your half sister . . .*

SUOR IMMACOLATA continued to make my life a misery, although it would have been miserable enough even without her. Santa Lucia felt like a prison, and I was surely a hostage. The food was only a little better than the scraps the Medici cooks threw to the dogs. Sharp straws poked through the mattress cover and scratched my skin, and vermin crawled out at night to feast on my flesh. Hot weather arrived, and my cell became an oven.

By early June of each year our household at Palazzo Medici had always moved from the city to one of the Medici country villas, most often to Poggio a Caiano, where mountain breezes cooled us on even the hottest days and Betta took me to wade in the Ombrone River that flowed past sprawling orchards and vineyards. Never before had I endured the sweltering days of summer in the city. But that summer of my eighth year there was no escape.

I begged Suora Madre—Mother Superior—to send for Aunt Clarissa. "Not possible," she told me coldly. "Accept the fate God has given you."

I LEARNED the rhythm of life at Santa Lucia by imitation, doing what the nuns did.

Seven times during a twenty-four-hour day, from before dawn until bedtime, a bell in the convent tower summoned the nuns to the chapel to chant psalms and prayers. The bells marked the canonical hours beginning with lauds while the stars were just beginning to fade, followed by prime at sunrise and then the "little hours" with the Latin names: terce, or third, at midmorning, sext— sixth—at noon, and the ninth hour, none, in midafternoon. Vespers was sung before suppertime, and compline before the start of the nighttime silence.

At first I had nothing to do in the periods between the prayers in the chapel. Then the mother superior decided that I must be put to work. She sent me to help in the washroom, stirring the household linens in great vats of steaming water with a wooden pole—work that had been done by slaves in Palazzo Medici. I hated it, but at least the nuns assigned there were not cruel, and one—Suor Caterina, who shared my name—was kind enough to explain the convent rules as we wrung out the sheets.

"Whatever you do, don't complain about anything," Suor Caterina warned me, twisting the linen one way as I twisted it the other. "One of the rules here is that anyone who complains will be punished. You'd be ordered to prostrate yourself on the stone floor for hours at a time."

I scratched a flea bite. "Just for saying the soup tastes like rotting garbage?"

Suor Caterina giggled. "Exactly. Even though you're right."

"No talking!" called the nun in charge.

For a few hours each day in the washroom my loneliness was lessened a little, when Suor Caterina and I managed to exchange a few words without being noticed.

Each night I pulled a straw through the mattress cover and hid it in a crack in the bed frame. When I had seven straws I tied them in a bundle with a thread drawn from the hem of my tunic. In this way I kept count of the weeks of my captivity as they dragged by. But no matter how earnestly I prayed for this nightmare to end, or for a visit from my aunt or a message from Betta, God remained deaf to my pleas. Maybe my desires weren't worthy of his notice. Or maybe *I* wasn't deserving of his graciousness. I began to lose hope.

Someone came to my cell when I was not there and found my bundles of straw. They were gone the next time I looked. I opened my *cassone* and saw that someone had taken my mother's ruby cross and my father's gold ring out of their silk wrappings and put them back carelessly, so I'd be sure to notice.

And always, there was the specter of Suor Immacolata, her eyes following me. I believed that she whispered her venom to the other nuns; they were watching me, too. I tried to avoid her, but that was often impossible. I looked for another place in the chapel to kneel during prayers, but there was none. She trapped me.

"You're hated here, you know," she hissed as we knelt for terce. "And not just because of your treacherous father. All the Medici are hated! Someone all of them will be driven out, murdered in their beds as they deserve. Florence will become a republic, and freedom will flourish once more."

I put my hands over my ears and refused to listen.

I'D LOST COUNT of the weeks I had been at Santa Lucia, but I could guess how many from changes in the weather. Early in September the rains came. At first they brought relief from the oppressive heat, but when they continued day after day, the dampness penetrated everything. Our clothes were always clammy. Mold flourished in every corner. We heard that the Arno River had overflowed its banks, sweeping off entire households.

Then the rains slackened and stopped. Chill winds swept down from the north, heralding the arrival of autumn and the coming of winter. I shivered through the cold nights with only a thin blanket, and soon I developed a persistent cough. The water froze in the washbasin. My lips were cracked and raw. My hands were bleeding.

I was not the only one who suffered. Suor Caterina, my friend in the laundry room—my *only* friend—became too sick to work. Many others had fallen ill as well, so many that the chapel was only half full at prayers. Then I learned that two of the sisters had died. One of them was Suor Caterina.

I wept harder at the news of the little nun's death than I had since my arrival at Santa Lucia. My despair deepened. No matter how tired I was, I couldn't sleep; no matter how hungry I felt, I couldn't eat.

Then one day the mother superior summoned me. "A gentleman has come to visit you," she informed me, sullenly. "This is against convent rules, but I am powerless to prevent it."

"Who is it, Suora Madre?" I asked, curious but also uneasy.

"Find out for yourself," she snapped.

She escorted me into a dismal parlor furnished with two crude wooden stools. A moth-eaten tapestry showing Our Lady with the infant Jesus hid some of the broken plaster of the walls, but there was no way to disguise the stained ceiling. A tall man in an elegant cape stood impatiently slapping his fine leather gloves against the palm of his hand. I had never seen him before. When I entered, the gentleman swept me a deep bow.

"*Mademoiselle,*" he said, and kissed my hand. I wondered if he noticed how rough it was. "*Signorina,*" he said, correcting himself with a smile, "I am the ambassador from France, representing His Excellency the king, François, on behalf of your late mother, Madeleine de la Tour d'Auvergne."

The ambassador bowed again and turned to the mother superior, who lurked stonily nearby, her hands tucked in the sleeves of her tunic. "If you would be so good, Suora Madre, as to give me some time in private with *la duchessina,*" he said politely.

The mother superior pursed her lips. "This is strictly against the rules, *signore,*" she said coldly.

His voice hardened. "It would be well for you to do as I ask, *madame!*"

The mother superior backed slowly away, and the ambassador's pleasant smile and kindly voice returned. He gestured for me to sit on one of the wooden stools, and he took the other, his long legs bent nearly double. "Now, Catherine—may I beg leave to call you by your proper French name?—tell me, *s'il vous plaît:* Are you all right here? Are you treated well? Because your mother was French, our king has an interest in your well-being. I understand that you were brought here for your own safety, due to the upheavals that are disturbing your city. But your father's sister, the good Signora Strozzi, wrote to me and asked that I intercede on your behalf and assure her that you are being properly cared for."

I remembered the convent rule: no complaining. I was afraid that if I told the ambassador anything about the wretchedness of this place, I would be found out. The best thing, I decided, was to remain silent.

The ambassador was looking me over carefully. I tried not to cough, but I couldn't suppress it.

"*Mademoiselle?*" he asked softly. "Catherine, will you answer me truthfully? Are you treated well here? You must trust me to help you."

I pressed my fingers to my chapped lips, imagining what would happen if the mother superior were listening. I wiped away first one tear and then another, but the effort of holding back was too much, and everything began to pour out of me—everything but the special kind of torment inflicted on me by Suor Immacolata and her hateful stories of my father.

The ambassador listened in silence, interrupting from time to time to ask a question or to have me repeat what I had said through muffled tears. When I finally finished my list of grievances, he touched my shoulder.

"Catherine," he murmured, "comfort yourself with the knowledge that this will end soon. I wish that I could offer you your freedom, but that's not within my power. Florence is in turmoil. Word has reached the city that Pope Clement paid a ransom of a quarter of a million ducats from the Vatican treasury and slipped away in disguise, rather than face the people of Rome. Hatred of the Medici increases daily, here as well as in Rome, and the mobs are truly frightening. Now the governors of the Signoria worry that you will come to harm. They don't want that. You're far too valuable to them as a hostage. But as the ambassador from France I'm in a position to insist that you be removed from this dreadful place and taken somewhere more pleasant where you will be protected."

I didn't understand all that the Frenchman told me, but I was willing to do whatever he asked.

We had been conversing in low murmurs, but now the ambassador said in a normal voice, raised slightly for the mother superior's benefit: "I'm pleased to see that you are well and content here, *mademoiselle*. Permit me to convey your greetings and your assurances to the governors of the Republic."

We rose from the two wobbly stools. I curtsied, and the ambassador bowed low over my hand and kissed it again. "Be ready to leave at any time," he whispered. "Do not lose faith." He called the mother superior, who appeared so quickly that I knew she had done her best to listen to our conversation. The ambassador thanked her for her courtesy and bid her good day.

As soon as the door was shut, the nun turned on me. "Why did he come here?" she demanded. "What did he want?"

"He came to see me because my mother was French, and therefore I am half French," I said. "He asked if I was learning my prayers, and I assured him that I was."

She knew I was lying. I could see that she was racking her brain to find a way to catch me in a betrayal. I met her probing look with a blank stare.

THREE DAYS WENT by with no word from the ambassador, and with each day my desolation increased. Had he forgotten his promise? Where did he plan to take me? Or had the Signoria decided that I must stay where I was as punishment for being a Medici?

Then, one night as I lay shivering on my straw mattress, the mother superior burst into my cell without bothering to knock. "Get up," she said in her grating voice. "You're leaving."

She dragged out from under my bed the clothes I had worn when the soldiers brought me there in May; it was now December. They were wrinkled and mildewed, but I put them on quickly. Clutching the *cassone* beneath my velvet cloak, I made my way alone to the portal. The mother superior had disappeared. Instead I found Suor Immacolata waiting for me.

I was so relieved to be leaving that I managed to find in my heart a little pity for the bitter nun. *"Addio,"* I said, as kindly as I could. "Good-bye."

She pulled open the door and shoved me through it. "A curse on you and all the Medici!" she cried, slamming the door shut behind me.

An iron bolt shot loudly into place. The night was moonless and very cold. I found myself alone in the darkness, quaking with fear.

I stifled a cry of alarm when the French ambassador stepped out of the shadows. He draped me in a black veil that covered me from head to foot, lifted me onto a waiting horse, and swung up into the saddle. Just before the veil fell over my face, I noticed two men armed with pistols riding with us.

"Hold tight, *mademoiselle*," the ambassador called over his shoulder, and I wrapped my free arm around his waist.

As we rushed off into the night, I thanked God that I was gone from that horrible place. It didn't occur to me then to pray that I would never return.

5

Le Murate

A FREEZING RAIN had begun to fall as we raced from Santa Lucia through the narrow streets of Florence. Occasional shouts sent a chill of fear through me. I buried my face against the ambassador's back, too frightened to speak. At last we halted. The men with pistols sprang off their mounts and lifted me down.

"Where are we?" I dared ask when I could find my voice.

"Santa-Maria Annunziata delle Murate," the ambassador explained. "They're waiting for you. Hurry, Catherine."

There were dozens upon dozens of convents in Florence, but, as it happened, I was acquainted with Le Murate. The abbess, Suor Margherita, was my godmother. Visitors were rare, and the nuns never left, once they'd been admitted through a hole symbolically broken in the wall and then sealed up again—Le Murate means "the walled-in ones." Goods were delivered into the convent on a wheel built into the wall, and sometimes unwanted babies, like Immacolata's, were left there, too. I'd gone there a few times with Aunt Clarissa to buy delicate sweetmeats for special feast days or a book of devotions to give to one of her close friends. She'd placed her order on the wheel and turned it, and then waited until the sweetmeats or the Book of Hours had been sent out.

Suor Margherita came to welcome me. The French ambassador leaped back on his horse and was gone before I could thank him. The abbess swept me inside, where several nuns were waiting to embrace me, though it was long past midnight. How different from the cold, sour greeting I had received at Santa Lucia!

"If only the governors had sent you here in the first place!" the abbess exclaimed as she led me to my quarters.

"But why didn't they?"

"Because you're a Medici, dear child. The governors want you safe but not comfortable. The French ambassador convinced them you'd be safer with us."

The rooms were simple but clean and pleasant. The bed had been made up with a thick mattress, warm blankets, and an embroidered satin coverlet. There was a plain but nicely finished wooden table and stool, and a prayer bench beneath a silver crucifix. Two paintings, one of the Annunciation and another of the Nativity, hung above the bed.

Adjoining my bedroom was a small alcove with a pallet

for the lay sister, Maddalena, who was to be my maidservant. Maddalena immediately filled a brazier with glowing coals and began to warm the linen sheets.

I placed the *cassone* on top of a larger chest. Suor Margherita smiled when she saw it. "A gift of our beloved Pope Leo," she said. "I remember it well."

The abbess kissed my forehead and wished me good night. Maddalena took my wrinkled and mildewed gown and cloak and brought me a soft linen shift for sleeping. Soon I was snug in my warm bed, settling down with a sigh of peace and contentment, the first in many months.

AT SANTA LUCIA I had grown thin and pale, my arms and legs were covered with scabbed vermin bites, and a lingering cough kept me awake at night. The abbess of Le Murate decided that I must be restored to health as quickly as possible. For the next few weeks I was petted and pampered, mostly at the hands of Maddalena, and I gave myself up to my servant's gentle care.

Every morning, as she carried in a basin of warm water to wash my hands and face and brushed my thick dark hair, I remembered the haunting story Suor Immacolata had told me about the infant she'd left at a convent and wondered about Maddalena. Questions began to trouble me: *Had the child been left here? And what about the other lay sisters who were our servants? Who were their parents? Was one of them my sister?* These were questions I couldn't ask anyone. But they were questions I couldn't seem to forget.

I had arrived at Le Murate during Advent, the month-long penitential season just before Christmas when the altars were hung with violet silk and everyone abstained from eating meat, eggs, milk, and cheese on certain days. Even with those regulations, the simple meals served in the large, bright refectory were delicious. The professed nuns ate first. When they'd finished, the young girls and a few elderly widows who made their home here entered for the second sitting. The novices and lay sisters ate last. The polished wooden benches and tables smelled of beeswax, and beautiful paintings of the Holy Virgin and the Christ Child hung on the whitewashed walls.

Within a week of my arrival, my strength returning, I began to explore my new home. In room after room, the nuns produced goods that were sold to support the convent. The scent of cinnamon drew me to the kitchen, where the sisters made sweets of honey and nuts and dried fruits, and there was a room where they filled pomander balls with dried rose petals and spices. Looms clattered in a weaving room, producing fine linen for altar cloths and damask tablecloths. Nuns stitched dainty sleeping shifts and undergarments of embroidered silk, trousseaux for wealthy girls about to be married. They spun fine gold thread for costly embroidery and worked delicate lace for vestments and altar hangings. When the bell rang in the tower, signaling the next hour for prayer, the nuns put down their work and hurried to the oratory. I went with them.

The chapel was close to the dormitories where the professed nuns slept, private spaces I'd been told were out of bounds to the rest of us. The door to one of these dormitories stood ajar, and, curious, I looked in when no one was around. At the end of the room stood an altar with a painting of the Annunciation, from which the convent took its name, Annunziata.

I knew that I should not go in there, but the calm face of the Virgin drew me to her, past the long rows of narrow cots made up with plain covers of unbleached wool. I knelt before the painting and gazed up at the scene: The Angel Gabriel has just told the Blessed Virgin that she will give birth to the Son of God. What must it have been like to receive such a piece of news? Mary had been just a young girl, like many at Le Murate. She must have been frightened, not knowing what was going to happen, having only her faith to sustain her. The Virgin would have understood how I often felt, swept along by events that I couldn't control.

My eyes were still fixed on Our Lady when I realized that I could no longer hear chanting. *How long ago had they stopped? Would I be missed? What if I were found here, where I didn't belong? When it was discovered that I'd broken a rule, would I be told to leave?*

Hearing footsteps, I dropped to the floor and wriggled

under the nearest cot. A plain wooden box took up much of the space. I pulled my knees up to my chest. My heart thumped much too loudly. Dozens of pairs of feet hurried by, but two pairs paused and entered. One pair soon left, but the other pair limped, one foot dragging, and stopped near where I lay. I squeezed my eyes shut, scarcely breathing, hoping the owner of the feet wouldn't see me. *Mary, Mother of God, help me.* After the nun had shuffled softly away again, I crept out of my hiding place, vowing to explore only the parts of the convent where I was allowed.

The week before Christmas I discovered the scriptorium. Here, in a series of small cubicles on the upper floor, a dozen nuns sat at slanted desks and copied manuscripts, missals and graduals and prayer books intended for private devotions. An elderly nun with gnarled fingers, her back twisted grotesquely, glanced up from her work and smiled. Her face was deeply seamed, but her eyes were a luminous blue green, shining with intelligence.

"I'm Suor Battista," she said. "And you are Duchessina, are you not?"

I said that I was.

"A child possessed with great curiosity, I believe."

I nodded, puzzled.

"I saw you hiding beneath my cot," she said.

I stared at the floor, ashamed. "I wanted to see the painting of the Annunciation. It was as if the Blessed Virgin was calling to me. I promise I won't do it again," I whispered.

"Of course you won't. And you're not supposed to be here, either, until you've finished your classes. But now that you are, let me show you the copyist's art. Silence, *per favore.*"

I stood behind her and watched her hand move unhesitatingly across the parchment, copying line after line of text, until the bell rang for prayer. "Will you teach me to do that?" I asked as we hurried to the oratory.

Suor Battista smiled. "Perhaps."

BY CHRISTMAS my cough had disappeared and my scabs were healed. The violet hangings on the altars were replaced with white damask embroidered with gold thread. During Mass in the convent church, the nuns sang in ethereal voices that I thought must be the way angels sounded. Afterward, the community of Le Murate feasted on roast meats and puddings as fine as anything I'd ever tasted at Palazzo Medici.

The next day I was allowed a brief visit from Aunt Clarissa. Convent rules prevented us from meeting face-to-face, but we could converse through the iron grille that separated those on the inside from those outside the convent wall. Although I couldn't see my aunt, it was a pleasure just to hear her voice again, to learn that her four sons were all well and that Betta had been taken into the Strozzi household to help look after the boys.

"I have wonderful news, Caterina," Clarissa murmured close to the grille. "I am again with child. Perhaps this time it will be a daughter!"

Naturally I rejoiced with her, although I felt a pang of jealousy: *I* had always been her daughter! *Will she forget me when she has one of her own?* I fretted.

Too soon the abbess signaled that the visit must end. I squeezed back tears.

"Don't cry, dear Caterina," my aunt said soothingly. "I shall come again, as soon as I'm allowed. But it will be difficult," she warned. "The Medici are hated more than ever. An angry mob attacked Michelangelo's magnificent sculpture of David in the Piazza dei Signoria, believing the statue is a symbol of the Medici! I can't leave the palazzo without an armed escort, although my husband opposes my going anywhere at all these days. But I wanted a chance to speak with my darling Caterina."

I recognized the dangers she faced. Over the past year I had been smuggled out of my home disguised as a boy, torn from my family's villa by soldiers, and rushed from one convent to another accompanied by men armed with pistols. "Be careful, Aunt," I begged. "I couldn't bear to lose you."

"Of course I will," she said.

Her footsteps faded away, and I wept unashamedly.

DURING THE JOYOUS yuletide observances that lasted through the Feast of the Epiphany, I got to know the other girls who lived under the care of the nuns of Le Murate. These were girls from wealthy families whose fathers wanted them to remain at the convent until their marriage had been arranged. Until their wedding day was near, they were not allowed to leave, even for a short visit.

Most of the girls suffered from a painful separation from their families and wanted desperately to go home. They longed to be with their mothers and little sisters not yet old enough to be sent to the convent. They missed their fathers and brothers, although the boys' lives were mostly separate from theirs. When I told them that I was happy to be at Le Murate, they stared at me, incredulous.

"But you're *la duchessina*!" exclaimed Niccolà, a slender, rather bold girl. "Everybody knows Caterina de' Medici is the richest girl in Florence, and the pope is your uncle. How can you like being *here*?"

"Because my mother and father are dead," I explained. "I have my aunt Clarissa, who loves me, but I didn't see her very often. My uncle the pope is far away in Rome and has no time to spend with me. Betta, my nurse, cares about me, but she has no say. Cardinal Passerini is supposed to be in charge of me, but I dislike him, and I'm sure he doesn't care about me. Before I came here, I was at Santa Lucia," I told the girls, "and they hated me. Here I feel safe, and the nuns are very kind."

"It's in the normal course of things for a young girl to leave her family," Giulietta, the oldest of my new friends, said knowingly. "Once the choice has been made for a girl—marriage vows or monastic vows—she no longer belongs to her family of birth. She belongs to her husband or to God. That's what my mother always told me."

"Do you really believe that, Giulietta?" asked serious-minded Tomassa.

"'One must accept it. It isn't easy, but it is life,'" Giulietta replied. "That's what my mother said, and I guess I believe her."

EPIPHANY HAD ALWAYS been my favorite feast day, celebrating the arrival of the wise men at the manger in Bethlehem. This year it reminded me of the chapel at Palazzo Medici with the frescoes of the journey of the magi. I wondered if I'd ever see the palace and those vivid paintings again, and I suffered a bout of missing my old life. Even the trays of pastries from the convent kitchen didn't cheer me. But then Giulietta sailed in with an announcement that excited us all.

"Beginning tomorrow, we're to be tutored in the virtues," she said. "We must learn how to conduct ourselves at all times in order to be proper wives. The nuns will instruct us."

"But how can the nuns teach us to behave like proper wives?" I asked. "What could they know about it?"

My question wasn't meant to be disrespectful, but my friends erupted in shy giggles.

The four of us, all recent arrivals at Le Murate, were

assigned to a class with several girls who had been there for some time and didn't pay much attention to the awkward newcomers. Instruction was conducted by Suor Paolina, whose beauty couldn't be hidden even by a nun's long tunic and veil. Her skin was smooth as ivory, her eyes the color of violets. Her slender fingers gestured as gracefully as birds in flight.

"Young ladies, your attention, *per favore,*" she said in a voice as silvery as a flute. "It is important that you discipline your body to move in only the most refined manner. You must walk at a measured pace and with a bearing that bespeaks the dignity of your gender and your station in life. Like this." Suor Paolina glided silkily across the room.

"It's as if she has wheels instead of feet," Niccolà whispered, not softly enough.

A tiny frown creased the nun's forehead. "Signorina Niccolà, *per favore,* let us see you walk from here to there."

Niccolà tried so hard to be dignified that she tripped over her own feet. The older, more experienced girls permitted themselves the hint of a smile, but I made the mistake of laughing out loud. The nun swiftly turned her attention to me.

"Signorina Caterina, the first thing *you* must learn is not to laugh in such a barbaric manner. Now, all of you, notice that my steps are never hasty, that my hands are lightly but firmly clasped and do not flap and wave about, that my eyes are lowered modestly, and that my mouth remains closed." Suor Paolina gazed steadily in my direction. The older girls smiled as though their lips were stitched together.

We new girls tried hard to do as we were instructed, but it didn't come easily. "Mouths closed *gently,* young ladies!" Suor Paolina reminded us. "Do not grimace!"

Tomassa seemed to possess effortless poise. Suor Paolina often used her as an example to the rest of us—especially me. I was short and still too thin, no matter how much I ate, and I was not naturally graceful. Giulietta, on the other hand, had trouble disciplining her eyes. Like me, she was always gazing about, and this brought constant reprimands from Suor Paolina.

"Do not regard anyone with your eyes, young ladies," Suor Paolina lectured us, although this was mostly aimed at Giulietta and me. "Keep them fixed and firm, lowered modestly. You must never, *ever* look at a man directly! Do you understand me?"

"But why not?" asked Niccolà, who already had made a reputation in the convent school for asking too many questions. They were often the questions I wanted to ask, but Niccolà saved me the trouble. "Why must we not look directly at a man?"

"Because your look is likely to inflame their carnal appetites, causing them to fall helplessly into sin. And surely, Signorina Niccolà, you would not want to be responsible for that!"

Niccolà had to agree that, indeed, she would not want such a thing. Afterward, though, we discussed among ourselves what Suor Paolina could possibly have meant.

"Lust," explained Giulietta, and we nodded knowingly, although we knew next to nothing about the subject.

We had much more to learn besides the virtues.

Suor Paolina accompanied us to our meals and turned her attention to our table manners. We had spoons for soup and knives to cut portions of bread and meat, which we ate using only the thumb and the first two fingers, then wiped our hands clean on a linen napkin. But now we were told that we must learn to use a fork, something new that had become accepted among the best families of Florence.

"It's essential that you learn to use a fork instead of your fingers," said Suor Paolina. "All it takes is practice."

"A *lot* of practice," Niccolà lamented, as a forkful of pigeon pie dropped into her lap.

The virtues were just one part of our training. Suor Rita was assigned to tutor us in arithmetic. "When you are mistresses of your own households, you'll need to know how to keep records of expenditures." I enjoyed arithmetic—there was something fascinating about numbers—and had already received some training from Fra Matteo at Palazzo Medici. But the others scowled through every lesson.

Suor Assunta tried hard to instruct us in the arts of needlework: spinning and weaving, which I found tedious but Tomassa took to immediately—"You don't have to think about it," she said. Sewing and embroidery seemed to be a pleasant way to pass the time, although I had small talent for it.

When the four of us were sent off to work on our stitchery, we found it an ideal time to discuss matters that we couldn't very well speak about in front of the nuns.

"Do you really think," Niccolà whispered, "that we can make men fall into sin? That we can inflame their carnal appetites just by *looking* at them?"

I hadn't any idea. Not quite nine, I was the youngest in the group and hadn't the advantage of growing up in a household with a mother and older sisters who might have imparted some basic knowledge of the ways of the world. But Giulietta had.

"Women are far more lustful than men," she informed us. My needle hung in midair, and I leaned closer in order not to miss a single syllable. "Everyone knows that. But we're also much stronger, and that's why it's up to us to keep men's passions under control. They can't resist us, you know."

I *didn't* know, but I found the subject interesting.

I thought of Suor Immacolata, the hateful nun at Santa Lucia, who claimed that my father had taken her virtue and left her with child. If she had been trained in the virtues, as we were being trained by Suor Paolina, surely nothing bad would have happened to her. Even if she had been a servant, she would have walked sedately, kept her hands still and her mouth closed, and—this was most important—she would have lowered her eyes and not inflamed my father's helpless lust. So it was not my poor father's fault that he had fallen into sin. It was the fault of the brazen servant who had led him there—or so I believed then.

WHILE I LIVED at Palazzo Medici and Fra Matteo was my tutor, he had abruptly stopped giving me instruction in reading.

"But why?" I'd asked, deeply disappointed.

"Cardinal Passerini's orders," he'd replied.

"But *why?*"

"I don't know, Duchessina. But I do know that you ask too many questions."

I'd taken my questions to Aunt Clarissa. The next time she'd gone with me for one of the cardinal's monthly inspections, she offered him her opinion.

"Surely, Reverend Father," she said, "you agree that it is entirely desirable that Caterina continue to develop the skill of reading. Undoubtedly it would stand her in good stead as she prepares for her future."

Passerini had shaken his head sternly. "Surely you understand, Signora Strozzi," he'd said in his arrogant manner, "that reading presents real dangers for women and girls?"

Wide-eyed, I'd looked from one to the other during this debate.

"I know of none," my aunt insisted stubbornly. "And for every danger, there is doubtless a positive good."

"You know nothing of the world, that much is clear," the cardinal had continued loftily. I thought he must be wrong about that; it seemed to me that my aunt knew a lot more than he thought she did. "A woman who can read is very likely to read the wrong things. I cannot allow such a corrupting influence."

"But surely, someone wise may guide her choices," my aunt had dared to argue.

"Reading is not wholesome for the pure minds of girls," the cardinal lectured her sternly. "Young women must heed only God and the will of their husbands! This ends our discussion. Good day, Signora Strozzi."

Aunt Clarissa had lost the argument, but it didn't really matter. Thanks to Fra Matteo, I could already read well, both Latin and the everyday Italian of Dante Alighieri, whose *Divine Comedy* I had studied before Cardinal Passerini had imposed the ban. Now, at Le Murate, I was pleased to learn that the nuns believed one must be able to read Latin in order to perform the Opus Dei—the work of God—at each of the devotional hours. Prayers and psalms were the heart of convent life. Reading, therefore, was essential.

Girls who'd had no previous tutoring—as most of them had not—were to receive their first reading lessons from the old priest who came to the convent church each day to say Mass. Not wanting to be left out, I went with them to stand at the iron grille. We listened as the priest on the other side mumbled each letter or combination of letters, and then tried to repeat after him, following along in a crude book. The lessons were very dull. It was a wonder anyone could learn that way, but somehow they did.

FAR MORE INTERESTING were the lessons I learned from Niccolà, Tomassa, and Giulietta. I listened as the girls chattered about their families, discussing the plans their fathers were making to marry them into this noble family or that one and the problems that came about as wealthy parents of young men demanded huge dowries from the brides' parents. I hadn't thought much about my future—I'd been too concerned with surviving the present—but now I began to wonder what might lie ahead for me. I mentioned this to my friends.

"Oh, don't worry," Giulietta said, dismissing my question with a wave. "Pope Clement has no doubt been shopping for a husband for you for years. You'll get a good one."

"And you're luckier than most of us," Tomassa sighed. "You're a Medici, and you've got heaps of money for a dowry." She pressed her knuckles to her lips. We all knew her story: Several ships owned by her father had been lost during a storm, leaving her with a dowry too small to attract a husband of her social class. "My father wants me to stay here and take the vows. The dowry is much less."

"Or no dowry at all," said Giulietta, who always seemed to know such things. "Like Suor Marta, the one who sings bass in the choir. I've heard that they let her come for nothing, because she has a beautiful singing voice as low as a man's."

Niccolà was sympathetic. "When my older sister married last year, Papa said it nearly bankrupted him. Now he has me to worry about. He's glad that his other children are boys."

I listened wide-eyed to these conversations. According to Aunt Clarissa, Pope Leo had been thinking of a proper husband for me when I was an infant. He had arranged the marriage of my parents, and he'd have done the same for me. But Pope Leo was dead, and Pope Clement was a different story.

What sort of husband does my uncle intend for me? I wondered. I couldn't imagine—but I *could* imagine the kind of husband *I* would want: someone like Ippolito.

6

The Scriptorium

EACH DAY AT Le Murate unfolded like the one before it, periods of study separated by prayers marking each of the canonical hours. I applied myself to my lessons. I struggled to master the virtues. I enjoyed a group of friends. And the nuns were good to me—perhaps too good, in the opinion of some.

"You're the nuns' pet, because you're a Medici," Giulietta said.

Everyone knew that my family had contributed many gifts to Le Murate. *Il Magnifico* had rebuilt parts of the convent once damaged by fire, and he'd donated several valuable paintings by Raphael and Leonardo da Vinci and other fine artists. Giulietta and some of the other girls were actually my distant cousins, but I was the only one who carried the Medici name. And I was the only *duchessina.*

It was the gift of a lute that had triggered Giulietta's jealous remark. I had mentioned one day to Suor Margherita that I'd once enjoyed playing the lute; scarcely a week later she saw to it that I had one.

I hadn't touched the instrument in so long that I had forgotten a lot of what I'd once learned. But I still remembered some of the simple tunes I'd played in the garden of Palazzo Medici during that brief, idyllic time when Ippolito had sat with me, singing the songs that I played.

The conversations of the other girls about marriage and the search for a proper husband had prompted me to think more and more about Ippolito. The more I thought about him, the more I yearned to see him again. True, he had deserted me when he ran away with the dreadful Alessandro and the hated Passerini. But, I told myself, surely he had no choice.

I often reimagined the scene in the stable at Palazzo Medici. In my new, much altered version of the event, Ippolito would refuse to leave and insist on staying behind to protect me. He, and not my aunt, would find a way to flee with me to Poggio a Caiano. Once there, he'd discover a little shelter down by the river and hide with me there, and the soldiers would never find me, and they'd give up and ride away without me. In my fantasy Ippolito and I would stay there, feasting on bread and cheese and wine brought to us by the kindly steward, picking grapes from the vineyard and fruit from the orchards until the danger had passed. Then we would ride together back to Florence and the Palazzo Medici, where life would go on as before, but without Alessandro and Passerini.

But, of course, that was not the way it had happened, and, as I plucked the strings of the lute, I wondered if I would ever see Ippolito again.

Giulietta was watching me. I handed her the lute. "Here," I said, "it's meant for all of us."

I HAD LIVED AT Le Murate for four months when I observed my ninth birthday on the thirteenth of April. A little more than two weeks later, on the twenty-ninth, the entire convent celebrated the Feast of Santa Caterina of Siena, my saint's day. Because Caterina was much beloved and many girls were named for her, the cooks prepared their most festive dishes in her honor. All day I hoped for a message from Aunt Clarissa, who had never failed to send me some small gift for my saint's day. I was even more thrilled when the abbess told me that my aunt had come to visit. It was her first since Christmas, when she'd told me she was expecting a child.

My aunt was waiting at the grille. Although I couldn't see her, I thought she sounded weary. I told her about my instruction in the virtues and in reading and arithmetic, knowing she would be pleased. I mentioned the lute.

"Then all's well with you here, Caterina?" she asked in a husky voice.

"It is. But I miss you so much, dear aunt," I told her, tears springing to my eyes. I wanted so badly to embrace her that I thrust my hand through the grille and tried to reach her. For a moment Aunt Clarissa's fingers touched mine.

"Then I shall not worry about you anymore," she said. "*Addio,* my child. Farewell."

Four days later Suor Margherita delivered the terrible news. "It grieves me to bring you this sadness, Duchessina," said the abbess. "Your aunt Clarissa died giving birth to a daughter. The infant also died soon after, but not before she had been christened Caterina, in your honor. On her deathbed Clarissa told her husband that she wanted you to have this." The abbess placed in my hands a rosary made of coral and pearls with a silver cross. I recognized the rosary from the many times I had knelt by Aunt Clarissa's side in the church of San Lorenzo, while she murmured *Ave Marias* and *Paternosters* and *Glorias*. I pressed the beads to my heart and realized the effort it must have cost my aunt to make her last visit to me.

The funeral mass for Clarissa Strozzi, sung by the beautiful voices of the choir nuns of Le Murate, offered no solace. My friends, Niccolà and Giulietta and Tomassa, tiptoed cautiously around me out of respect for my deep sorrow.

For days my head throbbed with the pain of my loss. For the first time I truly felt orphaned. Now I had no one at all.

THE ABBESS, believing that work and prayer were the best solace for an aching heart, soon decided that I had languished long enough. "I'm sending you to Suor Battista in the scriptorium. She specifically asked for you. You must have done something to impress her."

Unless they were teachers, like Suor Paolina and Suor Rita, professed nuns rarely had anything to do with the girls living at the convent. I had not spoken to the nun with the crooked back since I had happened upon her in the scriptorium soon after my arrival.

"The abbess sent me," I said, stepping into her cubicle.

"Good," said Suor Battista, regarding me with her luminous eyes. "Do you remember that you asked me on your last visit if I could teach you to do what I do?"

"*Sì, suora.*"

"Well, I'm going to try. I'm not the best copyist at Le Murate," she admitted. "Suor Agnese has the most elegant hand of any of us, and her books are most in demand, so she can't be spared for teaching." Suor Battista smiled. "But I am patient. That's my greatest virtue. Shall we begin?"

Before allowing me to form even a single letter, Suor Battista taught me first to use a small knife to prepare the goose quill, cutting the quill at an angle and shaping the nib. Then I learned to mix the ink from nutgall and a sort of gum. Finally, beginning on scraps of parchment already spoiled by a copyist's error, I made my first clumsy strokes.

It was true: Suor Battista was the very soul of patience. I quickly became tired of repeating the same strokes over and over, row after row of them. "You must do this until each stroke becomes a part of your hand," she said.

How dull, I thought. I longed to do something else—*anything* else—but the old nun kept me at my task.

When the lesson ended, Suor Battista showed me a copy of the Book of Hours being prepared for one of the convent's most demanding customers.

"This is Suor Agnese's work, ready to be bound. It has just come back from the illuminator, the artist who paints the miniatures in each book. We believe he's the best in the city." Reverently she turned the pages, past scenes from the Old Testament—Adam and Eve in paradise, Noah and his ark. "The patron wished to have a calendar included. Here's the painting for August, with the grape harvest. In the background you see one of the patron's country villas."

The brilliant colors leaped from the pages, the radiant blues made with ground lapis lazuli from Persia, a vivid green from crushed flowers, a vibrant red from the liquid of a certain insect. Gold leaf glowed in every little painting.

"Now the pages will be bound with embroidered velvet over boards, the clasps made of silver." Suor Battista smiled broadly, revealing a gap between her teeth. "They're so beautiful that I can hardly bear to let them go when they're finished."

At my next lesson I struggled to form the capital D of *Dominus* and the P of *Pax* and made a mess of both. "There must be an easier way," I grumbled.

"Oh, indeed there is. Decades ago a German artisan named Gutenberg invented something called a printing press. It's quite amazing, but to tell you the truth, Duchessina, I wouldn't want one of those printed books. Ours are so much more beautiful, and our patrons are willing to pay the price for that beauty."

I came to treasure the time I spent in the scriptorium with Suor Battista when I studied her art. Late that summer, after weeks of practicing on parchment, I had my first experience writing on vellum. "It is made from the skin of an unborn calf," Suor Battista explained. "Far superior to parchment, but very costly—only for someone as rich as *Il Magnifico*." She laughed to herself, remembering. "I knew him, you see."

I glanced up from the vellum sheet. "You did? My great-grandfather?"

"I did. *Il Magnifico* liked to gather the most talented artists and the most learned philosophers in Florence," she said, as we sat side by side at the slanted writing table. "It was an honor to be invited to dine with him, an honor that I enjoyed several times as a young woman. Once I was seated next to Michelangelo Buonarroti, while he was a student living at Palazzo Medici and working in *Il Magnifico*'s sculpture garden. *Il Magnifico* was greatly impressed by Michelangelo's talent. We had a fine conversation," she said, her blue green eyes twinkling.

"You knew him, too?" I asked, remembering the peculiar man who'd called me "little mouse."

"*Sì*, I did. He's a small man, you know, and rather ugly. I think he felt at ease with me. A beautiful woman would have made him nervous. My husband found this amusing."

Suor Battista watched patiently as I struggled to form an acceptable capital G in *Gloria*. I turned to look at her. "You were married?" I asked, unable to hide my surprise. A droplet of ink fell onto the vellum.

"I haven't always been a nun," she murmured. "But as a girl I was educated in this convent. Then I left to be married to a man much older than I. He was willing to overlook my crooked back because my father offered a large dowry. I was his third wife—his children were all older than I was!"

Hesitantly, I asked if she had had children.

"*Sì*." Suor Battista tapped the page, indicating that I was to continue my work. "I bore my husband three living children. When he died, they were taken by his family and my dowry was returned to me, as is the custom. With such a large dowry I could have married again, despite my appearance. But I didn't want to."

I glanced up from the page, where the letters were

beginning to swim before my eyes. "You didn't like being married?" I dared to ask.

"No, I confess that I did not. My husband was not a kind man, and he had a mistress whom he much preferred to me. I remembered how happy I had been here at Le Murate, and after his death I decided to come back and to take the vows."

I made another unsightly blot while attempting to copy a part of the Office for the Dead. "It's of no consequence," Suor Battista said. "This is how we learn—by making mistakes."

"But I make so many of them!" I complained.

"You're improving," she said. "I see progress every day. Now, shall we try again with the *D* of *Dies Irae*?"

ALTHOUGH THE older girls under the guardianship of the nuns at first paid scant attention to me, I eventually became acquainted with Argentina Soderini. Argentina was fifteen, and she had just learned that she was soon to be married. Argentina was the girl we all watched and secretly envied for her fair hair that fell below her shoulders. And she appeared to have been born knowing exactly how to keep her eyes modestly lowered and her voice pleasantly pitched. It seemed to Giulietta, Tomassa, Niccolà, and me that Argentina had been born a perfect lady, already in full command of all the virtues.

But we soon learned there was more to Argentina than

we imagined. It was Argentina who led us on midnight raids to the convent kitchen, Argentina who kept a supply of sweets hidden in her room, Argentina who'd once been infatuated with a groom in her father's stable and had even arranged to meet the boy for romantic trysts until she was caught. We younger girls listened with wide eyes and big ears.

"I'd never be able to get away with such a thing," said Cecilia, another of the older girls. "My nurse would have told my father in an instant if she suspected that I'd even allowed a boy's eyes to meet mine. Especially a servant's."

"That wasn't a problem," Argentina declared with a toss of her golden hair. "I simply made enough gifts to my poor, befuddled nurse that she turned a blind eye to some of my adventures."

"But still, you were found out!" Niccolà burst out, although it was understood that younger girls were permitted to listen but not to participate.

"*Sì,* eventually I was. That's when my father decided to send me here. I hoped that Giovanni would find a way to send me messages, but alas! He doesn't read or write, and even if he did it would have been impossible to exchange letters. But now all that's ended, and no doubt my Giovanni will marry some lusty peasant wench with a fat behind who'll provide him with a half dozen snot-nosed brats."

We were shocked by her manner of talking. This was our elegant Argentina? It was also one of the reasons we were drawn to her, because she dared to speak and act in ways we didn't have the courage even to contemplate.

One night, after she'd smuggled out a little wine from the nuns' cellar, Argentina decided to teach us to dance. I'd had no dancing lessons; neither, I found, had the other younger girls. But Argentina seemed to know all about it.

"The *bassadanza*," she explained, "is sort of a country dance, quiet and graceful, nothing very complicated, and the *pavana*, of course, is a court dance, very stately and dignified. Now, watch, ladies: This is the *sempio*, which is a single step. And—pay attention—the *doppio*, which is similar but lasts twice as long."

She demonstrated. We strived to imitate her.

"Come, ladies, follow me. First you rise onto your toes, like this—and then a step left, a step forward right, another step forward left, and then you sink down onto your heels."

Soon Argentina was leading her enthusiastic pupils around the room. From there we moved on to the *ripresa*—"*Bend* the knees, *feet* together, *up* on the toes, *again!*"—and putting it all together for the *voltatonda*, a full turn in place.

"This is the dance you'll be expected to perform at your wedding," Argentina advised us. "It's not too soon to start practicing."

It was only a matter of time until we were discovered. Argentina became bolder, and the nun in charge of the cellar noticed that several bottles of the best wine were missing. A novice was sent to keep an eye on the cellar. It might not have turned out so badly if the novice had simply reported to Suor Margherita that Argentina had helped herself to a bottle or two, but the novice then followed our friend to the refectory, where a party was being organized.

"We won't get caught," Argentina insisted, "as long as we don't make a lot of noise and we're out of here before lauds."

But of course we *did* make a lot of noise, and the novice ran off to awaken the abbess, who appeared suddenly in our midst, pounding on a table and shouting, "Young ladies! *Young ladies!*"

I had never seen her so angry; in fact, I had never seen her angry at all. The room went instantly quiet. I considered crawling under one of the long tables but dismissed that idea; I would take my punishment with the rest.

For ten days we were confined to our rooms, put on a strict fast, and required to kneel in the chapel without cushions and recite strings of penitential prayers. "You see," I muttered to Giulietta, "I'm *not* the pet. My Medici belly is just as empty as yours. And my knees really hurt."

When we had completed our penance, we learned to our sorrow that Argentina had been sent away from Le Murate in disgrace. We hadn't been given a chance to say good-bye.

THE HOT, DRY SUMMER that left the convent gardens parched was followed by the drenching rains of autumn.

Then the chill of winter settled in, and icy winds swept down from the north, sometimes bringing snow. I had been at Le Murate for more than a year. At last the warmth of spring sunshine drew us out of our cold rooms. In April of 1529 I was ten years old.

I generally remained ignorant of events in the world beyond the thick walls of Le Murate. No one spoke to me of what was happening in Florence or Rome or elsewhere, and I never thought to ask.

I had no visitors. Who would come? Perhaps Filippo Strozzi, Aunt Clarissa's husband, but he had never shown much interest in me, even before she died. On feast days the other girls spent brief moments at the grille with members of their family. At these times I deeply envied my friends—even Tomassa, whose visits were always fraught with difficulty as her father continued to insist that she must take monastic vows, become a nun, and spend the rest of her life in the convent.

"I have no vocation for it!" Tomassa sobbed after her parents had gone, and the girls had gathered in the parlor as we often did on Sundays and feast days. "I don't want to wear the nun's habit every day of my life and cut off all my hair and cover my head," she said, her eyes glittering with tears. Tomassa's pride was her thick, auburn hair that she had her maidservant brush for her every night. "And I've always dreamed of having children," she added with a sigh.

I tried to console her, but she wanted none of my sympathy. "You're a Medici, with all the money anyone could want!" she cried. "Not that it does you much good. Nobody in Florence wants to marry a Medici, even if you do have trunks filled with gold!"

Her bitter words stung me. They also made me angry, and my temper flared. "Yes, I am a Medici!" I said loud enough for everyone in the room to hear. I knew they were all staring at me, but I didn't care. "And you might be right—maybe nobody in Florence wants to marry a Medici. But not everyone in the world is so stupid, and someday I'll have a husband who is greater than anyone in this city. A prince—maybe even a king!"

I stormed out of the parlor, unwilling to let anyone know how hurt I felt. Aunt Clarissa had warned me that resentment of the Medici ran deep, and I had seen it for myself when we fled from Palazzo Medici. The mother superior of Santa Lucia had told me directly how much the Medici were hated, and I had experienced more than enough of the ill feeling against my family at that convent. But Tomassa's remark seemed more personal, designed to wound.

Later, when we were both calmer, Tomassa begged my forgiveness. I gave it, and in turn I begged hers. "Whatever my family is guilty of," I reminded her, "it is not my fault!" Then we embraced and kissed, but as we did, I wondered if we were truly friends.

7

Siege

THE MONTHS PASSED. Toward the end of the summer, as the blistering heat began to subside, the abbess gathered the entire community into the refectory after vespers. The long wooden tables had been taken apart and moved aside to make room for more than two hundred women and girls—the older ones packed together on benches, the younger ones standing along the walls. We waited silently for Suor Margherita to speak.

"We must prepare for difficult times," she announced somberly. "Early this summer the Holy Father in Rome reached an accord with King Charles of Spain. The pope promised to crown Charles as Holy Roman Emperor. In return, the Holy Father has been allowed to return to Rome."

Suor Margherita forced a thin smile and sighed. "Last

year during the sack of Rome, Florence declared itself a self-governing republic, free of the domination of the Medici." I bit my lip and kept my eyes fixed on the floor. "Pope Clement refuses to recognize the republic. He insists that Alessandro de' Medici will be made sovereign for life."

Alessandro? My dreadful cousin, ruler of Florence? A wave of dizziness swept over me. I put my hand out to steady myself against the wall. *If my uncle refuses to allow the people to govern themselves, why would he send Alessandro? Why not Ippolito?*

The abbess continued. "Alessandro is to marry Charles's illegitimate daughter, Margaret of Austria. Florence will be their wedding gift."

Feet shuffled, and there was a faint whispering. I felt eyes darting in my direction.

The abbess calmly explained that the members of the Signoria opposed Alessandro's rule but that my uncle was about to put the entire city under siege, to force the Signoria and the people of Florence to submit to his will. "Emperor Charles has promised to help the Holy Father compel us to accept Alessandro as sovereign. The emperor's armies have been ordered to surround our city and lay siege until we surrender."

No wonder the Medici are hated, I thought. I wanted to flee from the refectory to sort out my thoughts, but I didn't dare. I would have to stay where I was and suffer through this. Niccolà's warm hand grasped my cold one and squeezed it gently.

I couldn't bear to look at her, or at anyone, as the

abbess described plans being made to survive the siege. "Michelangelo Buonarroti, the great sculptor and painter and a native Florentine, has been summoned by the governors to design reinforcements of the city's defenses," she said. "And we have been warned to lay in additional food supplies. We shall begin at once to conserve our stores." Suor Margherita rose. "I entreat all of you to beg God's mercy during this difficult time."

The abbess swiftly left the refectory, followed by the professed nuns, then the novices, the widows, and finally the young girls.

Niccolà tried to reassure me. "It's not *you* they hate," she said. "But they've forgotten all the marvelous things that *Il Magnifico* did for Florence. After his death his son Piero ruined it all. My father says Piero was stupid and spoiled everything for everybody."

Piero was my grandfather, I thought; *my father's father.* All the hateful things Suor Immacolata had said to me about my father came rushing back, painful words echoing inside my head.

I freed my hand from Niccolà's grasp and rushed to my room. "Listen, Duchessina," she called after me. "I'll always be your friend. Even if you're a Medici."

OVER THE NEXT few weeks we watched food being delivered to the convent for storage: sacks of grain, barrels of dried fruit, slabs of salted meat, casks of oil and wine. The abbess, who regularly communicated with the world out-side the convent walls, again called the community to-gether to let us know what was happening. I dreaded this, fearing to hear even more condemnation of the Medici.

Her tone was unemotional. "Michelangelo Buonarroti has begun to rebuild the battlements around the city. It's hoped that these earthworks will be strong enough to resist the cannonballs the attackers will hurl at us. Workmen are digging deep trenches beyond the walls." But now the abbess's voice cracked. "The great artist has also ordered that everything between the city and the foothills be destroyed."

Everything destroyed? I heard the gasps of disbelief, and I remembered the man who had once disturbed me in the Chapel of the Magi. He'd seemed half mad then and com-pletely mad now.

"Everything," the abbess repeated. "Every farmhouse must be razed, every field and vineyard burned, every olive grove and orchard cut down. All of the villas are to be leveled, and the chapels, too."

Next to me Giulietta lowered her head and began to cry. Her family owned a beautiful villa just north of the city, on the winding road to Fiesole.

"You are no doubt wondering why such drastic mea-sures are being taken. Michelangelo insists it's the only way to deprive the attackers of protective cover and food sup-plies." Her voice became strong. "It is to be a fight to the death. We will not yield."

———

No matter how bad the news in the world outside our convent, nothing interfered with Suor Paolina's lessons in the virtues. The walls could be tumbling down around us, but we were to practice our needlework and play our lutes and remember to glide as we walked and to keep our eyes lowered and our voices carefully modulated. Our rations shrank, but we still ate our meager meals with our forks and used our napkins properly.

In mid-October we heard the first distant boom of the cannons. We all dropped what we were doing and rushed to the chapel to pray.

Be merciful to me, O God, be merciful, for I have taken refuge in you; in the shadow of your wings will I take refuge until this time of trouble has gone by.

We watched the autumn rains pour down in sheets in the cloister gardens. Water trickled through the workrooms on the main floor. On the top floor the roof leaked, damaging some of the precious books before we were able to carry them to a safer place.

In the refectory Suor Margherita told us, "The area between the ditch outside the city walls and the earthen battlements has turned into a bog, and the emperor's soldiers have given up the attack."

"Thanks be to God, we are saved!" cried one of the younger nuns, and the rest of us took up the cry.

Suor Margherita signaled for silence.

"No, dear sisters, we are not victorious. Far from it."

The abbess's voice was heavy with sadness. "When spring comes and the earth dries out, the soldiers will take up their positions and the bombardment will begin again. The farmers will not be able to sow their fields or replant their olive groves and vineyards. There will be no crops. Our stores will be exhausted. People will go hungry. The pope and the emperor are determined to starve us into surrender. Let us pray for strength and courage as well as God's mercy."

Starve us? How could my uncle do such a thing, just so that Alessandro can rule Florence?

We fell to our knees on the damp floor and recited the words of the twenty-seventh Psalm: *Though an army should encamp against me, yet my heart shall not be afraid. And though war should rise up against me, yet will I put my trust in him.*

For the first time in my life, I was ashamed to carry the name of Medici.

A BRUTAL WINTER descended on us. The soldiers had seized a number of forts along the Arno River, so that no supplies could be shipped up the river from the coast. This was the season of Advent, when fish was always served at least three times a week. Now we did without.

At Christmas we still had a plentiful store of grain and oil, but there were no fresh meats to roast on the spits in the kitchen, no soft cheeses for the lasagne. Instead, the cooks prepared *pasta e fagiole,* macaroni with white beans, seasoned with a little smoked ham, and we were grateful for it.

The Feast of the Epiphany was traditionally celebrated with cakes rich with eggs and studded with almonds. Now eggs were scarce, almonds rare. The citizens had always observed the feast day with a brilliant procession, the noblemen in velvet doublets embroidered with gold thread and pearls, hose with legs of different colors, and cloaks lined with fur, while the ladies watching from their palace windows were splendid in lustrous silks with jeweled garlands in their hair. There would be no procession this year, the abbess said.

In February, news reached Le Murate that Pope Clement had kept his promise to the Spanish king and set the iron crown of Charlemagne on Charles's head in the ancient cathedral in Bologna. Charles was now officially Holy Roman Emperor.

"The Holy Father can do what he wants for King Charles," the abbess told us, "but Florence will not surrender."

"We will not surrender!" we echoed.

We survived the winter, thanks to the convent's well-stocked larders and the cleverness of our cooks, but crowds gathered daily outside our thick walls, clamoring for food. The abbess ordered rations to be set aside for the needy from our own shrinking supply, but it was not nearly enough to satisfy their hunger.

In their misery they shouted insults: "Down with the Medici! You harbor the harlot within your walls! You feed her while we, the citizens of Florence, are left to starve!"

The abbess tried to protect me from such insults. But not all of the professed nuns and novices believed that I deserved protection. Most of them simply ignored me, averting their eyes. Nevertheless, I was aware of the whispers: *If Duchessina were turned out, sent elsewhere, perhaps our misery would be ended.*

There was nothing I could do. After months of contentment in my new home, I was as miserable as everyone else.

No more orders came to the convent for the Book of Hours or trousseaux or fine woven altar cloths embellished with lace. We mourned the death of the artist who painted the lovely miniatures in the books, who, we learned, had been killed by enemy soldiers as he tried to leave the city.

"We'll resume our work when our ordeal is over," Suor Battista assured me.

I wanted to believe her, but like many others, I was afraid we would not survive.

AS SPRING ADVANCED, there was an outbreak of plague in which many people in the city sickened and died. Hoping to prevent the seeds of the horrible disease from entering the convent, the nuns placed a bowl of vinegar near the alms basin by a slot in the wall through which people sometimes pushed coins. The sister in charge carefully rinsed the coins in the vinegar. A sour smell permeated the cloister.

Despite the precautions, members of our community began to fall ill. Their coughs echoed through the damp chambers. I, too, came down with a high fever, red spots on my chest, a cough, an ache in my limbs. When my strength continued to ebb away and I showed no signs of recovery, Suor Margherita sent for a physician. She described my symptoms to him through the grille and provided him with a vial of my urine. At his direction an apothecary concocted herbs and other secret ingredients that at first made me even sicker.

My sole visitor during my weeks of illness—aside from Maddalena, who was an attentive nurse—was Suor Battista. The old nun with the crooked back came daily to sit by my bed and tell me stories about *Il Magnifico* and the wonders of Florence during his lifetime. Fortunately, I was spared the Black Death, and slowly my health returned.

The siege continued, and the bombardment resumed. There was no more ham to flavor the beans and macaroni; then no more beans; finally, no more flour for macaroni. We existed on cabbage soup and some rotting carrots. The sisters planted vegetables in every available space, but the gardens couldn't yield enough to feed us all.

With little to eat, Suor Battista seemed to grow smaller. I went to sit with her in her cubicle in the scriptorium, although we did no copying, and she no longer told me stories of the Florence of her youth. Her strength ebbed. One day she didn't come to her cubicle, and I was told that she had taken to her bed. I waited until the nuns had gone to the chapel for vespers and slipped into the forbidden dormitory.

Suor Battista lay on her cot in her black tunic and white veil; professed nuns always slept fully dressed in their habits. She was not the only one in the dormitory— half a dozen others were also unable to get up. I tiptoed past them and knelt beside Suor Battista's cot. Her hands were folded on her breast, her eyes closed.

"Suor Battista," I whispered and touched a blue-veined hand.

Her eyes fluttered open. "Dear Duchessina," she sighed, a ghost of a smile on her lips. "Look in the box—" She stopped, her breath coming in ragged gasps.

"Don't speak." I laid my finger on her lips.

"In the box. Under the cot. Book. For you. Take. It."

"Later," I promised.

"Now. *Per favore.*"

I pulled the plain wooden box from under her cot— the box that had taken up so much space the time I tried to hide there. Inside was the Book of Hours with its glowing miniatures that she had often shown me.

"Yours. Take it," she said in a whisper so faint I had to strain to hear it. "Now go. Before . . . you . . . get caught . . . trespassing."

I promised to come back the next day, when the nuns were again at prayer.

But the next day the light in her blue green eyes had gone out, extinguished forever. I felt as though a light had gone out in my life as well.

Several days passed before a priest arrived to conduct the Office of the Dead, and when at last he did come, many of the sisters were too ill to attend or too weak to sing. I did my best to sing for her through my tears.

8

Escape

"DUCHESSINA!"

I awoke with a start. Someone was tapping on the door of my room, whispering urgently through the small iron grate.

"Duchessina!"

The abbess, I thought. Had I slept so soundly that I hadn't heard the bell calling us to prayer? I glanced up at the window high above my narrow bed. The night sky was black with a sprinkle of winking stars—still too early for lauds.

"Duchessina!"

The whisper grew louder, the tapping more insistent. The latch lifted and the door opened, letting in the bright glow of a candle, the rustle of skirts, the click of rosary beads. The abbess, dressed in her black mantle and white wimple, peered down at me. Her face was pale. "Get up and dress quickly. The soldiers have come to take you away."

"Take me where?"

"To another convent. The governors of the Republic have ordered you removed. They say you'll be safer. They've sent the soldiers to escort you. Silvestro Aldobrandini of the Signoria's Council of Ten is with them, and he has promised to protect you."

I was sure she didn't believe the promises she was repeating. She must have feared, as I did, that these men intended to harm me, maybe even murder me, once they'd gotten me away from Le Murate.

There was no need to ask *why:* It was hatred of my family, and especially of Pope Clement. At my uncle's orders the city had been under siege for nine months. Thousands had died of disease and starvation. The people of Florence were determined to take their anger out on someone. *On me.*

I shuddered, pulling the coverlet close, though the night was stiflingly hot. My teeth began to chatter, and I couldn't stop them. I was eleven years old, and for the third time in my life I was being forced to flee. This time, though, I might not be fleeing to safety but to my own death.

The abbess carried a candlestick. Her hands were clenched so tightly that her knuckles gleamed white in the candlelight. "Some men came earlier, just after we'd finished compline, and demanded to see you," she said, her dark eyes filled with worry. "I told them that the convent had entered the hours of silence. Now they've sent Aldobrandini with the soldiers. An angry mob has threatened to burn our convent to the ground if you remain here."

"Where do they say they're taking me?" I asked.

"To Santa Lucia," she said, avoiding my eye.

"Santa Lucia!" I cried, remembering the wretched months I'd spent there. "But that's a horrible place! I can't go back there! The mother superior, the nuns, the lay sisters, all of them despise the Medici, and me most of all."

The abbess touched my shoulder. "I'm aware of their feelings. But they are women of God, and I trust that they will protect you. You must endure this. It's your only hope, dear child. There is no other way."

I was trembling, but I tried hard not to show how afraid I was. I didn't want to leave Le Murate. I surely did not want to return to Santa Lucia. But more than that, I did not want to die. I didn't trust the soldiers not to turn me over to the furious crowd, and I had to think of a way to protect myself. "Very well, Suor Margherita," I said. "Give me a little time to get ready."

The good abbess kissed my forehead. "Hurry, Duchessina," she said.

I had the beginnings of a plan. If the crowd believed that I had become a nun, their religious beliefs wouldn't allow them to kill a bride of Christ. When the abbess had gone, I first whispered a prayer to the Holy Virgin and then rushed to the alcove adjoining my room where

Maddalena lay sleeping. I pulled back the curtain and shook her awake.

"Scissors," I said. "I need scissors—*now*, Maddalena."

She didn't ask why I was demanding scissors in the middle of the night. She flew immediately to the cupboard where our work baskets were kept.

"I want you to cut off my hair," I said. "All of it."

Maddalena stared at me. "But Signorina Duchessina," she stammered, "I . . . I cannot."

"You must," I insisted, "and quickly." When she still hesitated, I took the scissors from her, seized a hank of my long hair in one hand, and hacked it off. Maddalena gasped and clapped her hands over her mouth, watching me with horrified eyes, as though I had lost my senses.

I dropped the clump of hair on the stone floor and lopped off another handful. There was no mirror in my room, so I couldn't see what I was doing. "Here," I said impatiently. "Now cut, as short as possible. And then you must help me find a novice's habit. Who is a sound sleeper? Whose garb can we borrow without disturbing her?"

"Marietta," Maddalena said, reluctantly taking the scissors from my hand. "She sleeps as though she were made of wood." Still she hesitated. "But why must we do this to your beautiful hair?"

"Because the angry crowd out there may not believe that I am a nun, that I'm trying to fool them. If it comes to it, I will show them my naked head, and they will have to let me go."

Within minutes my servant had chopped my hair nearly to my scalp and slipped away to the dormitory where the novices slept on straw mattresses. While she was gone, I opened the miniature *cassone* with my most precious treasures: my mother's ruby cross, my father's gold ring, my aunt Clarissa's rosary, and now Suor Battista's Book of Hours—all mementos of the dead. I shut the box, making the decision to leave the *cassone* there, at Le Murate, rather than take it on such a dangerous journey.

Maddalena returned with Marietta's tunic and veil. "Signorina Duchessina, am I to come with you?" she asked as she helped me into the tunic. Her voice was brave, but I knew that she must be as frightened as I was.

I hesitated. The journey through narrow city streets would be far too dangerous. I wanted her company, but I feared for her life almost as much as I feared for my own. "No, Maddalena, they won't allow it. I'll send for you later," I promised, although I knew it was an empty promise.

Maddalena had finished arranging the white veil over the stubble of my hair and knelt to fasten the straps of my sandals when we heard another anxious tapping at the door of my cell. "Duchessina? You must hurry! The men are restless, and they're growing angry at the delay. A dozen of the sisters are blocking the door, but they can't hold off the mob if they're determined to enter."

"The *cassone*," Maddalena whispered, handing me the wooden chest of treasures.

"No," I said. "*Per favore,* ask Suor Margherita to keep it

safe for me." I paused at the door and asked Maddalena the questions that had been simmering since I'd first come to Le Murate: "Who are your parents? How did you come here?"

Maddalena stared at me, puzzled. "My father was a stonecutter. He worked for Michelangelo and died in an accident before I was born. My mother was a peasant's daughter."

"Did she leave you here on the wheel?" I asked.

"No. She died when I was small, and my grandmother brought me here. They were very old and poor. Why?"

"No reason." I sighed with relief—this was not Immacolata's child—and flung open the door. "I'm ready," I said.

The abbess stepped back, eyes wide, fingers to her lips. "Duchessina? Is it you?"

"Yes, Reverend Mother, it is. Now please take me to these officers, and let them see what they're about to do."

I was afraid the abbess would refuse to let me use this disguise, even to save my life, but she simply bowed her head for a moment and then turned and walked swiftly across the dimly lit courtyard. Led by the sound of her sandals slapping softly on the stone floor, I followed her toward the heavy oaken door.

I could hear the loud voices of men on the other side of the thick walls. The promises of their leader didn't reassure me. I didn't trust him, yet there was no one else to trust. I could only pray that Signor Aldobrandini was a gentleman true to his word and that he did not intend to kill me as soon as he had taken me from the safety of the convent. Or even worse, to turn me over to the soldiers to do with me as they wished.

I was just eleven years old, and I did not want to die!

The abbess glanced at me, and I clenched my teeth and nodded. She drew back two sets of bolts, and the low, narrow door, rarely opened, swung inward on creaking iron hinges. I hadn't left this sheltered place since I'd arrived three years earlier. I stepped over the high stone sill, into the menacing world outside the convent walls. The sky had begun to lighten; soon the nuns would be gathered in the chapel, chanting lauds, but now several of them stood with arms linked, facing the crowd and blocking the entry with their bodies.

I glanced at the band of eight soldiers, grumbling among themselves. In front of them stood an elegantly dressed man in a crimson cloak trimmed with ermine; this I took to be Silvestro Aldobrandini. *Not so frightening,* I thought. But beyond the soldiers and their leader I could make out the dark silhouettes of a gathering crowd and hear the murmurs that grew suddenly more threatening. The crowd surged forward. The soldiers ordered them back, but not all obeyed. The man in the crimson cloak approached, leading a mule.

Suor Margherita hugged me fiercely, kissed me on both cheeks, and blessed me with the sign of the cross. The brave nuns, murmuring prayers, parted and allowed me to pass but quickly closed ranks against the threatening crowd. *"Miserere mei, Deus,"* they prayed. "Have mercy on me, O God, according to your loving kindness . . ."

The man in the crimson cloak gaped at me. He was clearly expecting a young duchess, not a nun, and did not know what to make of what he saw. "Duchessina?" he asked uncertainly.

I drew in my breath and let it out again. I had to go through with my plan. "Will you dare remove me now?" I called out boldly. "And show yourself to the people carrying a nun from her cell? I will not go with you quietly, as you expect. Let us see who will dare to drag a bride of Christ from her convent!"

I felt a little sorry for Aldobrandini. He had been given an order, and now he was finding it hard to carry it out. Clutching his feathered hat, he knelt at my feet. I wondered if he could guess how terrified I was.

"My dear Duchessina," he began, "I am here, not of my own will, but by order of the governors of the city of Florence." He stammered out his proposal: We would proceed immediately to the convent of Santa Lucia, where I was to remain until the siege of the city was lifted. "With God as my witness, I will guarantee your safety as long as you are under my protection," he said. "The good nuns agree that you will be safer at Santa Lucia than you are here. The crowd behind me has threatened to burn down Le Murate, but I believe that when they see you as you are now, no harm will come to you or to the nuns of Le Murate."

I prayed that he was right. The nuns had protected me by taking me in, and now I must protect them by leaving. Signor Aldobrandini helped me to mount the mule. I flinched when I heard the oaken door close firmly and the sound of the two iron bolts being shot into place. I wanted to weep, to turn back, but I couldn't allow myself to show how frightened I felt. Chin lifted defiantly, I began the journey, Signor Aldobrandini leading my mule through the angry mob. When they surged toward me, their faces hate filled and mouths twisted with poisonous rage, I pulled back my veil, revealing my shorn head. Muttering, the mob fell back, and I passed through without further incident.

Aldobrandini handed me down from the mule when we arrived at Santa Lucia, and, relieved to have survived the crowd's fury, I thanked him for his protection.

"I salute you, Duchessina," Aldobrandini replied. "You are a courageous young woman." With those words, which I never forgot, he led the soldiers away.

I WAS NOT WANTED at Santa Lucia; Suora Madre made that plain the moment I walked through the door. "We're taking you only because the governors have ordered it," she said. "And surely you don't expect us to believe that you've become a nun."

"I expect nothing, Suora Madre," I said, and I made my way alone back to my old cell.

I pitied the nuns, who seemed even more starved, more wretched than those at Le Murate. The mother superior was no longer pudding faced but skeleton thin. Still, each day the nuns who had survived observed the devotional hours, just as they always had. I joined them. Suor Immacolata, who had made my life so miserable before, was not there.

"Dead," the nuns replied when I asked. "The plague."

The mother superior told us nothing of what was happening beyond the convent walls. Perhaps she didn't know. Perhaps she was too weak from hunger to care. It was hard to care about anything when our stomachs were empty. Then, on the twelfth of August, after I'd been at Santa Lucia for three weeks, word came that the siege had ended. Suora Madre wept when she announced that the resistance had collapsed, the governors surrendered. Michelangelo's fortifications had withstood the bombardment, but at least sixteen thousand citizens of Florence were dead from illness and starvation. Pope Clement had triumphed. His supporters were again in control of the city.

Two days later I asked the mother superior for permission to return to Le Murate. "Go back to your Medici lovers, and good riddance," she said, barely glancing at me. "It's one less mouth to feed."

"I'll need an escort," I said. "The streets are unsafe."

"Then I suggest you go the way you came—disguised as a nun," she said.

And so I did, dressed in the novice's tunic and veil, riding the mule the abbess managed to find for me. The poor animal was nothing but skin and bone, as starved as the peasant who led him. The menacing crowds were gone, Via Larga nearly deserted except for a few wretched souls begging for food. No one paid any attention to a lone nun on a skinny mule.

"There will be something for you to eat at Le Murate," I promised the peasant, whom I now recognized as the gardener at Santa Lucia. I hoped I could make good on my promise.

I was welcomed back to Le Murate with tears of joy. My three good friends embraced me, once they'd gotten over the shock of my shorn hair, and wanted to know everything that had happened to me since they'd last seen me. Maddalena fell on her knees to thank the Blessed Virgin for my safe return before I sent her off to find a bit of food for the peasant, still waiting at the gate.

My immense relief and pleasure at being among those I loved didn't last long. The Medici were again in power. I should have been pleased—this was my family, after all—but I was not. Every promise the pope had made to the Florentines was quickly broken.

Pope Clement announced that the republic was finished and gave the order to destroy the great bell that hung in the tower in the Piazza dei Signoria. Known as La Vacca, "the cow," because of its deep tolling, the bell had rung to summon generations of young Florentine men to the piazza. "The sweet sound of liberty, silenced forever," wept Niccolà.

Suor Margherita made the announcement in the refectory: The pope declared that Alessandro de' Medici would be installed as sovereign lord and absolute ruler of Florence, once proper arrangements had been made. I could not imagine anything worse than living under Alessandro's rule.

There is one more thing, the abbess added. The pope had called for the arrest, torture, and execution of the members of the governors' Council of Ten. That included Silvestro Aldobrandini.

After we'd been dismissed, I rushed to Suor Margherita's chambers. "Signor Aldobrandini does not deserve to be put to death!" I told her. "He saved my life."

"Then ask His Holiness to spare him," she said simply.

In my old cubicle in the scriptorium I prepared quill and ink and sat down to write, addressing the letter to His Holiness, Pope Clement VII. In the fine hand that Suor Battista had worked so patiently to teach me, I wrote my defense of Aldobrandini, the passionate words flowing from my pen.

"I beg Your Excellency's mercy for this noble gentleman's service in the protection of your grateful relative," I wrote. I hesitated; should I add something else? No, I decided, there was nothing more to say. With a flourish I added my signature, *Caterina de' Medici, Duchess of Urbino.*

Then I sprinkled the wet ink with sand, folded the letter, and asked the abbess to have it sent to Rome by fastest courier.

WEEKS PASSED with no reply. I stayed with the nuns of Le Murate, having no other place to go and no desire to leave them again. I learned that the Palazzo Medici was virtually deserted. Cardinal Passerini, who had fled with Alessandro and Ippolito three years earlier, was dead, a victim of the plague. Alessandro was in Rome with the pope, preparing to take control of Florence. No one seemed to know where Ippolito had gone.

Although the siege had ended and the gates of the city were again open, life remained hard. Gradually, though, food was brought to Florence from other parts of Tuscany—olive oil and grain and preserved meat. But there were no fresh fruits or vegetables, eggs or cheese. All the fields surrounding Florence had been destroyed, even beyond the margins ordered by Michelangelo. The besieging armies themselves must have gone hungry.

In mid-September I received a letter from Rome. Nervously I took it to my bedchamber and opened it. "We have considered your request regarding Silvestro Aldobrandini, lately of the Council of Ten, and we are pleased to inform you that his death sentence has been commuted to lifelong exile."

My words had touched their mark. I had saved Aldo-brandini's life. I sat holding the letter, enjoying the feeling of triumph.

But the letter continued. "Now that it is once again safe to travel, you are to begin preparations immediately to remove with all haste to Rome, where you will make your home under our loving guidance."

The letter was signed *Clemens Pater Patrum VII*— Clement, Father of Fathers, VII.

I stared blankly at the letter in my lap.

My life was about to undergo another enormous shift. The last thing I wanted to do was move to Rome to be with Pope Clement, but I had no choice but to obey. Destiny had called me again.

9

The Road to Rome

THE FIRST CHALLENGE in preparing to leave for Rome was gathering the proper clothes. I had arrived at Le Murate with only my wrinkled silk gown and a mildewed velvet cloak. The gown had fit me when I was eight years old, but now I was eleven. For most of the past three years I had dressed nearly every day in the drab gray tunic and underskirt required of the girls at the convent. On feast days we were allowed to dress up. I'd managed to squeeze into my old gown that the nuns in the sewing room had cleaned and let out and added to as I'd grown, disguising the seams with clever embroidery stitches. Then, due to the effects of the siege and the terrible shortage of food, I'd become quite thin. Now the old silk gown hung on me, worn out and ill fitting. I could not go to Rome in that dress or in the tunic and underskirt.

Suor Margherita dispatched a letter by courier to the pope, assuring the Holy Father that I looked forward with eagerness to the honor of being in his presence. Then she added that, as impatiently as I wished to be on my way, my present wardrobe was unsuitable. I would need several new gowns, she wrote, as well as cloaks and undergarments, hosiery and slippers.

The pope replied, telling her to provide whatever I needed. The problem was that he sent no money. The abbess instructed the seamstresses to do what they could with what they had. From their store of silks and damasks used to make vestments for priests and bishops, they fashioned a gown of green brocade, embroidered the bodice with gold thread and edged the white sleeves in lace; they also made me a plain russet dress for traveling. Nuns who'd specialized in creating exquisite bridal trousseaux for the daughters of rich patrons stitched new sleeping shifts and undergarments of fine linen. Cecilia, one of the older girls who would soon leave the convent to be married, made me a gift of a pair of slippers that she'd outgrown.

Niccolà, Giulietta, and Tomassa watched these preparations with mixed feelings. "It's not fair!" Giulietta complained. "No sooner do you come back to us so that we can be together again than you tell us you're leaving."

"I feel sorry for you, Duchessina," Niccolà said bluntly.

"How can you bear to make your home with the pope, after what he has done to our city?"

"How can I not?" I asked. "I have no more choice than the citizens of Florence do. When the Holy Father speaks, I must obey."

"She's right," Tomassa remarked to Niccolà. "Duchessina has no more choice than *we* do."

"And what about your cousin, Alessandro?" asked Giulietta. "He's to become the lord of Florence. Will we like him, do you think?"

"No," I answered frankly. "You won't. He was a cruel boy, and I doubt that he's changed for the better, now that he's a man."

It would be much different if it were Ippolito, I thought, but didn't say.

BEFORE I LEFT FLORENCE, I wanted to see Filippo Strozzi to ask a favor. In reply to my request, Clarissa's former slave, Minna, came to accompany me to Palazzo Strozzi. Filippo greeted me somberly. He'd sent his three younger sons with Betta to the country before the siege began, while he and his oldest boy, Piero, had remained in Florence. All had survived and were now reunited in the city, including Betta.

This was the first time I'd seen my uncle since before Clarissa's death, and I was shocked by how much he had aged, his face deeply lined, his eyes hooded and grave.

I began to weep as though the news of her death were still fresh, but Filippo remained stoic, muttering, "God's will be done."

He summoned his sons to the grand receiving room, once the scene of many festive entertainments but now stripped of its rich tapestries and furnishings. The boys' faces were thin and sad, and they had little to say. But at that moment Betta sailed in, and the mood changed. Unlike the Strozzi father and sons, she was used to expressing her feelings. The barren receiving room echoed with her wails of grief for my dead aunt and cries of joy at the sight of me. Soon everyone was laughing and crying and talking at once.

When the excitement settled down, I spoke to Filippo. "The Holy Father has called me to Rome. He's sending a cardinal with an escort to accompany me. I've come to ask if you'll allow Betta to return to my service and travel to Rome with me." I turned to Betta. "If she's willing."

Betta didn't wait for Filippo Strozzi to signal his opinion one way or the other. She threw her arms around me again, burying my face in her pillowy bosom until I was half smothered. Filippo forced a thin smile. "Certainly Elisabetta may go with you to Rome. God protect you on your travels."

ON THE MORNING of October first, my few belongings, including my precious *cassone* with its treasures, were packed in panniers slung over the back of a donkey. I said good-bye to Maddalena and my friends at Le Murate, promising that my visit to Rome was only just a visit and that I expected to return to Florence before long. We kissed one another, and wept, and kissed again. Suor Margherita gave me her blessing. My three best friends presented a going-away gift—a very pretty head covering they had taken turns stitching in secret.

My feelings that day were a tangle: I was sad to be leaving my dear friends and uneasy about what my life would be like under the pope's thumb, but I was also thrilled by the notion of a journey to a faraway city. Except for my earliest years, of which I had no memory, I had never traveled outside of Tuscany. I'd spent the past three years shut up in one convent or another, and I was curious about Rome. I had heard much about its ancient ruins, as well as about St. Peter's Cathedral and the Sistine Chapel, and the Palazzo Vaticano, the pope's palace. I wanted to see it all.

With Betta and four armed guards I rode off to join our traveling party on the piazza outside the monastery of San Marco. A short and jowly cardinal with bulging eyes was waiting for me, surrounded by several assistants, a number of servants, and Swiss Guards from the pope's private army. He'd also brought us two well-fed mules for the journey.

"I am Cardinal Giovanni Salviati, nephew of the late Pope Leo," he said. "My mother, Lucrezia Salviati, is Pope

Leo's older sister. You will make your home with her, as you did when you were an infant."

"Cardinal Giovanni seems kindly," I murmured to Betta as the procession prepared to move out.

"Everyone seems kindly at first," she said drily.

A band of musicians played, drawing a small crowd to the piazza. It was meant to be a festive occasion, but the mood remained dark. The crowd watched sullenly as we rode down the Via Larga and past the Palazzo Medici, now empty and shuttered. On every building the Medici coat of arms with the seven balls, called *palle,* had been defaced or destroyed.

"It's not like it was once," muttered Betta. "There would have been cheering throngs whenever a Medici rode through the streets of this city. *'Palle, palle!'* the people used to shout."

But there was no cheering now for the Medici *duchessina* and a Medici cardinal. I stared straight ahead, relieved that there were no shouted insults, no hurled garbage. When our entourage crossed the Arno, I turned back for a final view of the Duomo, the red-tiled dome of the great cathedral gleaming in the midmorning sunlight. Then I set my sights forward, toward Rome.

MY EXCITEMENT dimmed as the hours passed and the journey grew long and exhausting. We stopped each night at monasteries along the way, where we were fed a simple meal, given plain beds, and sent along our way in the morning under stormy skies. On the fourth day we reached the Porta Flaminia and entered Rome in a down-pour. Cardinal Giovanni led the way to the Piazza Navona in the heart of the city and the stately palazzo nearby.

I climbed down from the wooden seat on the mule's back. Liveried guards opened the massive door, and I stepped inside the great central courtyard decorated with marble statues, many of them beheaded or completely smashed. An elderly woman in a velvet gown of several vivid colors slowly descended the broad staircase. She was short and heavy bodied, her face round with sagging chins and protruding eyes—clearly a Medici. Jewels shone around her neck and on her wrists and sparkled on every finger, so that she seemed half buried in ornaments. Once she'd looked me over, a smile brightened the deep grooves of her homely face.

"I am Lucrezia de' Medici Salviati, your great-aunt," she said in a warm and pleasant voice. "I welcome you once again to Palazzo Medici. The last time I saw you, you were little more than an infant, and now you're a fine young lady! I hope you will be happy here."

Aunt Lucrezia led the way up the broad stairs from the courtyard to the *piano nobíle,* and then, breathing hard, up a narrower stairway. Betta came along behind us carrying my little *cassone,* and a servant followed with the rest of my belongings. There wasn't much.

"We're fortunate to be alive," Lucrezia said, as she

showed me to my apartment. "The palazzo was attacked and looted during the sack of Rome. As you can see, it was badly damaged and nearly everything destroyed or stolen. By luck, we were away at our country villa, and I had my jewels with me." She stroked her pearl and sapphire necklace. "How my dear brother, the late Pope Leo, would have wept to witness the ruin of the most glorious city in all Christendom."

I remembered the night the young cleric and the old priest had come to the Palazzo Medici in Florence and repeated stories of rape, murder, thievery, and destruction in faraway Rome. We hadn't realized then how our own city was about to suffer. In both cases, the blame lay on Pope Clement and Emperor Charles.

Over the next day or two, while I rested and began to find my way around the battered palazzo, Betta befriended the servants and delivered a report on the large household, which seemed to include dozens of people. It would have taken me a week or more to find out what Betta managed to extract in a matter of hours.

"Lucrezia's husband, Jacopo Salviati, is old and ill and seldom leaves his rooms," said Betta. "Her son, Cardinal Giovanni, and his assistants spend most of their time at the Vatican. Her widowed daughter, Maria, lives here— she always dresses in mourning. A younger daughter, Francesca, was about to marry a distant Medici cousin in Florence, but the wedding has been postponed because of the siege. Francesca is in a black mood. You'll see for yourself soon enough—you're to take your main meal each day with Lucrezia and her daughters. The women eat together, separate from the men, and Lucrezia usually invites her friends to join her."

Equipped with this information, I prepared for my first dinner at the Roman palazzo. Betta helped me dress in my new green gown and fastened my mother's ruby cross around my neck. "What shall we do about your hair, Duchessina?" she asked. It hadn't been quite three months since I'd cut it all off, and Betta hadn't recovered from her first sight of my bare head.

"Perhaps I should simply go as I am," I teased her. "To make a memorable first impression."

"Let's leave that for the *second* impression," she said briskly. "Or maybe the last." She began arranging the head covering my friends had given me, taking care to hide stray hair ends, and sent me off to dinner.

They were waiting for me. Lucrezia and a half dozen ladies in sumptuous gowns and masses of jewels all smiled pleasantly. Among them was a younger woman, remarkable in a plain black gown with a simple white head covering and no jewels of any kind—*Maria, the widow,* I thought. A beautiful girl wearing a lovely blue gown and a dark scowl stood apart from the others. *That must be Francesca, the disappointed bride.*

"Welcome, Duchessina," said my aunt. I curtsied, and the meal began.

Listening to the conversation at Lucrezia's dinner, I

concluded that nearly every lady at the table was of Medici blood or had married some Medici cousin. That made me wonder about Ippolito. I hadn't seen him for three years. Possibly he was in Rome. Very likely someone at this table knew where. Someone might even mention his name. I listened carefully, waiting for a chance to ask about him that would seem entirely natural, one cousin inquiring after another. But as the days passed, I learned nothing, not even from Betta.

My favorite in the household was Maria Salviati. My great-aunt Lucrezia was always pleasant, but she was interested almost exclusively in her lady friends, who were polite to me but distant. Gloomy Francesca seemed interested almost exclusively in herself. Only Maria, who wore sadness as habitually as she wore her widow's weeds, took much of an interest in me.

"I have a son just your age. Cosimo will soon be twelve," she told me. "But I rarely see him." When I asked where he was, she replied, "With his father's family, of course, as he has been since my husband's death." She studied her long, thin fingers and finally managed a wan smile. "If you are in need of anything at all, Duchessina, come to me. I should be glad to help you."

It was the custom in Rome to serve certain dishes on certain days of the week: macaroni dressed with a meat sauce on Thursdays, fish stew or ravioli stuffed with cheese on Fridays, and saltimbocca or some other veal dish on Saturdays. This custom seemed odd to me, but whatever was served was well prepared and plentiful, and it had been a long time since I'd had enough to eat. So, with no idea what else was expected of me, I ate my fill and waited to hear from Pope Clement.

ABOUT A WEEK after my arrival in Rome a papal messenger delivered a note. His Holiness would receive me at dinner in three days at the Belvedere, his private villa near the Vatican. I took the note to Maria.

"You'll have frequent dinners with His Holiness," Maria said. "And I've been thinking about this: You have only one proper gown. It's pretty, but it's not enough— you've worn it every day since you arrived. I'll summon a tailor and a seamstress to begin work on a larger wardrobe. The bigger problem is your hair." Maria rarely smiled, but the sight of it actually made her laugh. "What a disaster!" Maria declared. "It will be Easter until you can go about without a head covering."

On the appointed day I anxiously dressed for dinner with the pope in my green gown. Betta fussed over me, adjusting the sleeves. Lucrezia loaned me some jewels. Maria arranged the headdress my friends had made.

"Are you nervous?" she asked when I dropped a ring for the third time.

"*Sì*," I admitted. "A little."

"Don't be. There's nothing to be uneasy about," she assured me. "My mother and sister and I will be with you.

There's sure to be a huge crowd. No one will pay the least attention to you."

The sky was a perfect blue, and autumn sunshine bathed the buildings of Rome in a warm glow as we set out toward the Vatican, accompanied by a dozen servants.

"It's a nuisance," Francesca grumbled, riding beside me on a handsome gray mule. "The dinners are terribly dull, but we have to go. My mother is the pope's official hostess."

Our party skirted the Piazza Navona and made its way along a well-traveled street of half-ruined palaces. We crossed the Tiber by way of a graceful bridge, passed the Castel Sant' Angelo and the walls of the Vatican, and arrived at the Belvedere.

I hadn't seen Pope Clement, the man I remembered as Cardinal Giulio, since he'd ridden out of Florence in a gala procession on his way to Rome. I was just six years old then; now I was eleven and a half, and I believed I'd become quite a different person. My experiences at Santa Lucia and Le Murate had taught me much. Surely the Holy Father would notice the changes in me and be pleased.

I followed Lucrezia and her daughters along a crimson carpet. One set of doors after another parted, opened by white-gloved Swiss Guards in blue and yellow striped uniforms with red doublets, the Medici colors. We passed through room after room hung with rich tapestries and works of art, having no chance to admire any of it. Instead, I kept my mind on the lessons that Suor Paolina had drilled into us:

Eyes lowered modestly.

Hands still, clasped lightly.

Sedate walk, neither quick nor laggardly.

Thoughts quiet, reflective.

I failed that fourth lesson completely. I could discipline my body—hands, feet, even my eyes—but my mind raced unrestrained in every direction.

The last set of doors swung open. A tall, gray-bearded figure in white robes trimmed in gold was seated on a dais upon a high gilded throne, his feet resting on white silk cushions with gold tassels. He was surrounded by cardinals in scarlet from hat to slippers, bishops in purple, and men and women in splendid clothes and marvelous jewels, all watching as we made our entrance, one by one.

A page announced first Lucrezia, then Maria, followed by Francesca. I watched carefully as each of the women stepped forward, mounted the red-carpeted steps to kneel before the pope, kissed his feet, and then kissed the ring on the hand he extended. The pope smiled and nodded, and one of his cardinals helped each lady to her feet. I knew exactly what to do.

Next it was my turn: "Caterina Maria Romula di Lorenzo de' Medici, Duchess of Urbino!" intoned the page. I moved forward—*eyes lowered, hands still*—until the moment that I would kneel and bend to kiss the pope's feet.

But Pope Clement rose abruptly from his gilded throne, thrusting aside the tasseled cushions, and threw his arms open wide. "Our dearest Duchessina!" the pope cried.

Surprised by this move, I glanced up. Tears glistened in the pope's eyes, and while I stared openmouthed, breaking every rule Suor Paolina had tried so hard to instill in me, the tears began to course down the Holy Father's whiskered cheeks.

"How happy we are to see our dear niece once again," he proclaimed in a deep voice loud enough for everyone in the enormous chamber to hear. And then he clasped me tightly, my face muffled against his snow-white robes.

What do I do now? I wondered, quite breathless.

The pope released me from his embrace. I dropped to my knees, pressed my lips on the white slipper, reached for the hand with the gold Ring of the Fisherman symbolizing Saint Peter, and kissed it. One of the cardinals prepared to raise me up, but the pope brushed him away and did me the honor himself.

Pope Clement did not allow me to step aside. He kept me next to him, and even when we were escorted into the grand dining hall with long tables laid for a hundred guests or more, he led me to a place near the papal chair. *You got through a vicious mob,* I told myself; *certainly you can get through this.*

The table was set with square crystal goblets rimmed with gold; silver plates displaying the papal seal inlaid in gold; and silver knives, spoons, and forks bearing the Medici crest. This was a huge step from dining in the convent refectory with girls my own age or even eating with Lucrezia's ladies. I decided that it would be better to eat nothing, rather than risk making some dreadful mistake that Suor Paolina had not prepared me for. Surely she couldn't have known about all of this! And I had lost sight of Aunt Lucrezia and her daughters.

Over the next several hours the meal proceeded with course after course—I stopped counting when I'd passed twenty—each presented by a liveried footman, first to Pope Clement and then to his honored guests, which included me. Soon the Holy Father seemed to forget about me, hunger overcame me, and I began to sample the various dishes, wielding the fork with growing confidence.

While the pope was occupied with his friends or signaling for his goblet of wine to be refilled, I glanced around the vast hall, my curiosity overcoming all the cautions I'd been given about keeping my eyes lowered. How would I ever find out what was going on if I could only stare at my plate?

My eyes swept the great hall. Everyone was engaged with the food, the wine, their conversations. A small orchestra—a harpsichord, a harp, three large violas, two lutes—provided music, although people talked so loudly I can't imagine they could hear it. I was listening to the music when I noticed a young man with finely chiseled features, standing to one side. He was dressed magnificently in a jeweled doublet and silk hose, one leg yellow and one red; his dark hair curled nearly to his shoulders.

I recognized him at once. *Ippolito!*

I gasped and stared, willing him to look at me, until at last our eyes met. He nodded and smiled slightly. I half rose, wanting to rush to his side but forcing myself to do no such foolish thing. Gazing after him, I sank back onto my seat and watched him disappear behind a pillar near the orchestra.

A woman seated beside me spoke up. "Signorina, I've asked you a question," she said crossly. I begged her pardon.

"I asked if you're enjoying your stay here in the Eternal City," she repeated.

"Oh, indeed, *signora!*" I said, much too enthusiastically. "I know that I shall love it here!"

THE POPE'S elaborate dinner lasted for several hours. Riding back to Palazzo Medici beside Maria, I considered how to bring up the subject that had me in such turmoil. Finally, I simply blurted it out: "I saw my cousin, Ippolito, at the dinner. Does he live nearby?"

"*Sì*, quite nearby," she replied. "Ippolito and Alessandro both live at the palazzo. But we hardly ever see them."

"They live at Palazzo Medici?" I echoed stupidly. "Both of them?

"*Sì*. Ippolito is also my cousin, the natural son of Giuliano, my mother's brother—Leo's brother, too, of course.

And Alessandro is here because he's Clement's favorite." Not noticing my agitation, Maria added, "They're cousins, they've grown up together, but it seems they're not fond of each other. Their disagreements have become much worse since the Holy Father made it known that he's preparing Alessandro to rule Florence in the very near future."

"But why Alessandro? Ippolito is older," I argued. "He should be the one to rule, shouldn't he? He's much beloved by the people of Florence."

"You may be right, Duchessina. Ippolito would no doubt agree with you, and I know it was Pope Leo's intention—he spoke of it often. But that's not what Pope Clement has decided."

This is not the way it should be, I thought stubbornly. *Someday Ippolito will rule Florence.* Then, for the first time, another thought came to me: *And I will be at his side.*

10

Ippolito

POPE CLEMENT ALWAYS insisted on calling himself my uncle, although our relationship was not close; we were only very distant cousins. After our first emotional meeting, my "uncle"—or whatever he was—paid little attention to me. He informed me of his wishes through Cardinal Giovanni Salviati.

"The Holy Father has decided that you must acquire a number of necessary skills, Duchessina," said the cardinal. "These will prepare you for your eventual marriage to a nobleman who would expect certain talents in a wife."

Various tutors would be assigned as needed, he explained—one for Latin, who would also instruct me in Greek; and a mathematician to introduce me to the study of astrology. The needlework skills and "the virtues" I'd acquired at Le Murate were deemed sufficient.

But, I wondered, what sort of man would expect his wife to have such an education? Passerini had insisted to Aunt Clarissa that women should not be taught to read. Why had this changed?

"His Holiness gives no reason," said the cardinal. Then he asked, "Can you ride horseback?"

"A little."

"You must learn to use a sidesaddle," he said.

It was the custom for ladies to ride a horse or mule facing sideways on a wooden seat strapped to the animal's back, while a groom led it at a walking pace. Why, then, did I need to learn this new style?

"His Holiness gives no reason," repeated the cardinal.

How exasperating! Apparently I wasn't to be given an explanation for anything. "Who will teach me?"

"Your cousin, Alessandro."

"Alessandro? But that's impossible!" I cried.

The cardinal merely lifted his eyebrows. "It is as His Holiness wishes. Alessandro seems pleased by his assignment. Perhaps it will come to please you as well, Duchessina."

I rushed to Maria to complain, telling her how unhappy I was with this arrangement. "Alessandro used to enjoy tormenting me," I told her.

"Maybe he's improved. Anyhow, it is as His Holiness

wishes," Maria said, sounding like the cardinal. "Wait, I have a gift for you." She handed me some sort of linen garment, the like of which I'd never seen. "Short under-breeches gathered at the knee, to wear beneath your petticoat when you go riding, for modesty's sake, in the event you fall off."

Glumly, I prepared for my first lesson and dragged my feet to the palazzo stables by the Piazza Navona, trailed by my usual company of Lucrezia's friends who chaperoned me while mostly gossiping among themselves. Alessandro was waiting for me, sprawled on a bench. He didn't bother to rise.

At nineteen, Alessandro was tall and thin. A few straggly hairs sprouted on his chin, and his teeth were as pointed as a rat's. He wore a permanent scowl, his eyes bored and half closed. He greeted me with a croak, imitating a frog.

"Hail to the Frog Duchess! You don't mind if I call you that, do you? Because you know it's true." He looked me over, his lip curled disdainfully. "So it has become my duty—no, my extreme pleasure—to teach the Frog Duchess to ride a horse."

I stood rooted to the spot, forcing myself to be still. My throat was dry, but I managed to speak. "I'm sure you'll find me an apt pupil," I said. To my horror my voice *did* come out like a croak.

Alessandro called sharply for the groom to bring my

horse, a pretty mare. Her leather saddle was equipped with a high pommel and two stirrups hanging to one side. She looked much taller than the dainty mules I was used to. The groom boosted me into the saddle and instructed me to hook my right leg around the pommel. I was grateful for the linen breeches.

My feet had scarcely found the stirrups before Alessandro leaped onto his gray stallion and trotted off. My horse followed. The stallion broke into a gallop; my mare did, too. We tore through the Campo dei Fiori with its bustling market, knocking over baskets of fruit and fish, alarming housemaids doing their shopping, setting dogs off barking. We clattered over the Ponte Sisto across the Tiber to Trastevere, a neighborhood of poor merchants and craftsmen, plunged down the narrow streets, and emerged at last in the countryside. I hung on desperately, not daring to look back to see what had happened to the ladies who were supposed to accompany us. Although I was still rather small and thin, I was agile, and after a time I began to get the feel of horse and saddle.

"Not bad for a Frog Duchess," Alessandro muttered darkly when we'd passed the ashen-faced ladies at full gallop and returned to the stables. "Scared, weren't you?"

"Not in the least," I lied, although my body ached from head to foot. Even if I had fallen off and shattered every bone in my body, I would not have admitted any fear to Alessandro.

"Then I must try harder next time," he said over his shoulder, tossing the reins to a groom and swaggering off.

POPE CLEMENT required my presence at many of the elaborate dinners at his villa, Belvedere, or at his private apartment in Castel Sant' Angelo. I made the short trip between the Palazzo Medici and the pope's residences two or three times each week with Lucrezia, the pope's official hostess. Sometimes Maria or moody Francesca came along.

Advent began on the fourth Sunday before Christmas. At Le Murate we'd abstained from meat, eggs, and cheese during this period. I was surprised, then, that Pope Clement's Advent dinners were as luxurious as ever, with stuffed capon and wild boar, as well as quantities of wine and exquisite sweets.

When I asked Francesca why the Holy Father didn't observe the Advent fast, she shrugged. "He's the pope. He can eat whatever he wants."

By Christmas I had still not exchanged a single word with Ippolito, although I thought about him all the time. Every dinner at the Belvedere was an opportunity to look for him. If I had a glimpse of him, and if he actually looked my way and smiled, I counted the dinner a success, no matter what wheezing old bishop or shrill-voiced countess sat next to me and claimed my attention. If I didn't see him, I brooded for days, until the next opportunity.

Whenever I thought of Ippolito, I indulged in fanciful

dreams of the future. Now twenty-one years old, ten years older than I, Ippolito had grown into a handsome man with intense dark eyes and a warm, bright smile. Watching him from far off, I believed I saw in him a good-humored zest for life. Surely, I reasoned, Ippolito would come to rule Florence, as Pope Leo had planned it before his death. The idea had even occurred to me that one day we might marry. But even as I nurtured these notions, I knew they were no more substantial than the morning fog: Regardless of what Pope Leo had intended years ago, Pope Clement had promised Florence to Alessandro and his future bride, the emperor's daughter.

But that doesn't mean we can't marry, I thought. *And maybe in time the Holy Father will see that Alessandro isn't suited—or worthy— to rule Florence, and that Ippolito is.* I clung to that hope as though wishing could make it true.

ALTHOUGH I WAS rarely alone, I was often lonely. Betta was the one steadfast connection to my childhood, but the gap between us widened as I grew older. Lucrezia treated me kindly enough, but she was caught up in her own affairs and often seemed distracted. Francesca's moods were unpredictable, merry one day and glum the next as her plans to wed Ottavio kept changing. Pope Clement exercised complete control over my life, and I was often in his presence, but I was never alone with him—not once.

"The Holy Father watches over you from afar," Cardinal Giovanni told me piously, "just as the angels on high watch over every one of us."

I didn't think Pope Clement could be compared to an angel, but Alessandro, on the other hand, did resemble one of those ugly demons that crawled up out of the depths of hell in religious paintings. Our gallops through the countryside had become wilder, but I got more confident at taking jumps over streams and logs; I learned to trust my horse, although I never trusted my cousin. Then, as winter closed in, my riding lessons came to a temporary end. "Until spring, dear little Frog Duchess," said Alessandro with a mocking bow.

The one person in whom I could confide was Maria, but not even to Maria could I speak of my feelings for Ippolito and my dream of returning to Florence with him as his wife. I was afraid she would tell me I was being childish.

DURING THE FIRST blustery months of 1531, I spent most of the day with my tutors in the library of the Palazzo Medici. The library had been established by Pope Leo, and he had continued to add to it even after he'd moved to the Vatican. After his death, much of his collection had been brought back to the family palace. Oddly, it had somehow survived the sack of Rome. Now it was seldom used. A fine layer of dust covered everything, the candles in the wall sconces were burned to the sockets, and the fire in the stove had been dead for a long time. When my lessons began, Lucrezia ordered the candles replaced and the fire lit. Here the mathematician spread his zodiac charts, and the tutor in Latin and Greek found books to suit his purpose. When the tutors had gone for the day, I thought of the library as my own private refuge, filled with treasures to be admired and mysteries to be explored.

On a high shelf reached by a ladder, I discovered a portfolio containing a number of drawings of an elephant; some were in red chalk on gray paper, others were pen and ink sketches on parchment. According to notes in the portfolio, the elephant, named Hanno, had been a gift from the king of Portugal to Leo. Pope Leo had kept Hanno in an enclosure within the Vatican walls. I felt I had something in common with Hanno—the poor elephant must have been lonely, too. I moved the portfolio to a lower shelf where I could reach it easily.

One day I arrived in the library and was startled to find someone already there, seated at the table near the window where I always sat.

It was Ippolito.

"Duchessina!" he exclaimed, leaping to his feet. "How I've wanted to talk to you, ever since I learned you were here!"

I thought I heard in his voice what I was feeling in my heart. "I've wanted to talk to you, too," I said. "Why are you here?"

"I'm working on a translation from Latin of the *Aeneid,*

about the fall of Troy. I'm not sure I'm up to the task, although I do write a little poetry. And you, Duchessina? Some serious study for you, as well?"

"I've come to study the pope's elephant," I said, immediately wondering why I'd said something so foolish.

"Ah, you've learned about Hanno. Well, whatever reason brings you here, I'm glad of it," he said. A smile lit Ippolito's handsome face. I smiled back at him.

We spread the drawings on the table, and together we examined them.

"Everyone in Rome has heard of the great beast," Ippolito said. "Leo loved him, the Romans loved him. Hanno was always at the head of the pope's processions through the city. But Hanno died after he'd been with our uncle for only two years. That was before you were born. Pope Leo was deeply saddened. Of all the animals in the Vatican menagerie, the elephant was his favorite."

"Hanno must have been magnificent," I said. "I've never seen an elephant."

"Nor have I. I was in Florence then, but even there he was talked about."

Discussing an animal that neither of us had ever seen: That was how our childhood friendship began to grow into something so much more.

THROUGHOUT THE WINTER Ippolito and I met whenever we could at the library—it was not often—always

careful to keep our meetings secret. The secrecy was Ippolito's idea. "I'm quite certain the Holy Father would not
consider me a proper companion for *la duchessina*," he said.
We took turns pulling volumes down from the shelves
and studying them, using that as an opportunity to sit so
close that our heads nearly touched. I can scarcely remember what we talked about—perhaps our days in Florence, perhaps our still formless dreams of the future. It
didn't matter. I was with Ippolito.

On the Tuesday before the beginning of Lent we spoke
for the first time of our feelings.

"I'm not quite twelve years old," I told Ippolito, "and
yet I've lost nearly everyone close to me: my father, my
mother, my aunt Clarissa, my grandmother, my great-
uncle Pope Leo, Suor Battista at Le Murate—all people
who truly cared what became of me. I wanted to stay
at the convent, because I have friends there and the abbess is my godmother, but Pope Clement ordered me to
come here. Aunt Lucrezia is kind to me, and I've become
fond of Maria, and yet I'm lonely. Do you understand,
Ippolito?"

"Of course I understand, Duchessina. Pope Leo became like a father to me, after my own father died. He
used to take me hunting when I was just a little boy, before he became pope. Now I, too, have no one. Clement
assigns me a hundred duties to perform, yet I'm as lonely
as you are."

"But you have Alessandro," I suggested.

"Alessandro hates me!" Ippolito exclaimed. "And I feel the same about him. But we must hide our real feelings."

"I hate him, too," I said heatedly. "Alessandro calls me the Frog Duchess. He mocks me. I sometimes thought he would manage to kill me during those terrifying riding lessons."

"But you have the pope's protection. The Holy Father gives every sign that you are cherished."

"I want to believe that Pope Clement loves me, but in my heart I know the truth: He only *pretends* to love me. His affection for me is as feigned as yours for Alessandro."

Ippolito shook his head sadly. "Clement doesn't even bother pretending for me. Not only does he have no affection for me, he'll do whatever he can to get me out of the way. Then Alessandro will have it all."

"But why?" I asked. "Alessandro is cruel and bad mannered, so why—"

"Because Alessandro is Pope Clement's bastard son!" Ippolito interrupted. "And that's why he's the favorite, and why he will one day rule Florence. You didn't know that?"

"No," I said, shocked. "I knew that Alessandro's father was a cardinal, but I believed that he was the son of Cardinal Passerini."

"You had the wrong cardinal in mind, Duchessina."

Ippolito's hand had come to rest on mine. My heart was pounding so hard that I believed surely he could hear it. But then he caught himself and drew away.

I changed the subject quickly. "The frescoes in the Chapel of the Magi," I said. "Do you remember them, Ippolito?"

"Of course I do, my dear Duchessina," he said softly. *My dear Duchessina!* I could have wept with joy.

"I used to go to the chapel often," I rushed on, the words tumbling out. "I'd make believe that I was actually in the picture, riding a fine white horse in the procession."

Ippolito laughed and reached again for my hand. "And which member of the crowd were you?" he asked. My fingers curled around his.

"I used to imagine myself as a little girl riding quietly off to one side. But now I believe I'd be a wise woman, taking my place with the three wise men. That would be interesting, don't you think?"

Ippolito gazed at me thoughtfully. "You, a wise woman? You are indeed a most unusual girl, Duchessina," he murmured.

I met his gaze—just what we had been cautioned not to do by Suor Paolina—and wondered if he would take advantage of this opportunity to lift my hand to his lips and kiss it. *Oh, do, dear Ippolito!* I begged silently.

Ippolito bent closer. We were so intent on each other that neither of us heard the door of the library open. My fingertips were near Ippolito's lips—I could feel his warm breath—when raucous laughter erupted behind us, startling us rudely.

"Well, well, well!" roared the awful Alessandro. "What

have we here? Have I happened on a tender moment with our little Frog Duchess? *Per favore,* don't let me interrupt!" Alessandro slouched carelessly on a bench, propped his feet on the table, and leered at us. "As you were saying, Ippolito? Do continue your speech, cousin."

I was too stunned to utter a sound, but Ippolito quickly found his voice. "Duchessina and I have been investigating the stories of the Vatican menagerie collected by our uncle, Pope Leo. Duchessina is especially curious about Hanno."

"So the frog is now in love with the elephant, is she?" He squinted, looking from Ippolito to me and back again with heavy-lidded eyes. "No doubt the Holy Father would be interested to hear this."

"And I doubt he'd be in the least interested," I said, speaking up suddenly.

Alessandro grinned. "You're wrong about that, Duchessina. The thing he cares about most is finding you the perfect husband. Have you heard the list? Any number of fine gentlemen are willing enough to marry a Frog Duchess if her dowry is large enough. Shall I tick them off? Start with the Duke of Sforza, missing all of his teeth and most of his manhood. Philibert, Prince of Orange, who led the enemy troops against Florence, topped the list of suitors until he took a bullet in the head during the siege. Shall I go on? No?" Alessandro rose lazily and made a mocking bow. "Then I wish a good day to you both." He saluted insolently and sauntered out of the library.

Ippolito was white with anger. "He will certainly report to the pope what he believes he's seen here today. And the Holy Father will do whatever he can to prevent us from being together. We must not meet again until it's safe, Duchessina," he said, adding sadly, "and it may never be."

I nodded dumbly and ran off in tears, my hopes fading like smoke.

THERE WERE NO MORE chance meetings and only glimpses of each other at the pope's entertainments. My studies did little to distract me from my unhappiness. Lent began, and Pope Clement suspended his dinners.

On Easter morning Pope Clement was carried on a gilded throne from the Palazzo Vaticano through the narrow streets of Rome to the cathedral church of San Giovanni in Laterano, where he would celebrate the Easter mass. Crowds of ordinary people jammed the streets, while highborn gentlemen and ladies—including Lucrezia and her daughters—watched from the balconies and windows of palazzos along the winding route. I was with them. Every churchman of any importance was a part of the procession, along with musicians and choirs and jugglers and tumblers, and all of the Swiss Guards, followed by select members of the nobility on horseback. Alessandro was among them, on his prancing gray stallion. Ippolito, riding much farther back in the procession, passed directly beneath the balcony where I was standing.

He didn't look up. Leaning out for a better view, I watched him until he was out of sight.

A few days after Easter I received an invitation to a festive dinner at Castel Sant' Angelo. For the first time I was appearing without a concealing head covering. Maria had arranged my hair, still quite short, with a garland of jewels. I had another new gown, this one of rose damask. The light of hundreds of candles shimmered on the gilded walls.

I ignored Alessandro, seated far away from me, but could not resist gazing often in Ippolito's direction. Once—only once—he glanced my way. He didn't smile, but something in his look lifted my heart. I had a feeling that soon we might meet again. Maybe there was a glimmer of hope after all.

My attention was claimed by the Frenchman on my left, Cardinal Gramont, who peppered me with questions in Latin until Pope Clement called for the attention of his guests. The busy hum of voices died away. "We are pleased to make to this distinguished audience an announcement concerning the appointment of a new cardinal to our Sacred College," said the pontiff in his sonorous voice.

Murmurs of speculation rippled among the dinner guests. A pope had the privilege of naming as many cardinals as he wished. The important families in Rome and Florence courted the pope's favor, sometimes with large gifts to his treasury, hoping that one of their sons might wear a cardinal's red hat. Many of the guests that day were surely expecting one of their own to be chosen.

"It gives us great pleasure to inform you that the man to be so honored is one greatly beloved by us," continued Pope Clement. "The scarlet hat of the cardinal will be presented to our dear nephew, Ippolito de' Medici, dedicated to the service of God."

Ippolito, a cardinal? How could that be—he wasn't even a priest!

I gasped, "No!" I felt the blood drain from my face and thought I would faint. *Not this!* my heart cried. *Now he'll never be mine!*

The French cardinal looked at me curiously and asked if I were unwell. "It's nothing," I assured him, although in fact it was everything.

Ippolito rose and approached the dais where the pope was enthroned. Cardinal Gramont applauded enthusiastically; I forced myself to join in with the others. Ippolito had never looked more handsome, more intelligent, more winning. He knelt before Pope Clement and kissed first the pontiff's feet and then the Ring of the Fisherman.

My head swam, and, pressing a starched white napkin to my mouth, I struggled to breathe normally. I'm not sure how I managed to get through the next few hours.

I had no one in whom to confide my misery—not even Maria. Although I still felt quite unwell, I joined Lucrezia and her friends at dinner the next day. The conversation at the table startled me. The ladies were discussing Ippolito's elevation to the College of Cardinals.

"What can His Holiness be thinking?" demanded one woman, her fingers so laden with jeweled rings that she managed a fork with difficulty. "Imagine, deciding that such a handsome young man would enjoy devoting his life to the church! Why, I hear that he's only twenty-one, extraordinarily young to be made a cardinal, and not even ordained a priest!"

"And has no desire whatsoever to become a priest, from what I can tell," a second lady offered. "What a pity! My youngest daughter would have made him a splendid wife, if he'd so chosen."

I stared at my plate, afraid my eyes would betray me, hoping the ladies wouldn't notice my trembling hands.

"And so gifted!" caroled a third. "Plays the lute, expert on the organ, a talented poet, a fine athlete—"

"A priest can take pleasure in all of that, as can a cardinal, and even a pope," Lucrezia interrupted. "My brother was pope for eight years before his untimely death and cardinal for many years before that, and I daresay he enjoyed every moment of his life."

I glanced up. The tone of the conversation had taken on an unaccustomed edge.

"'God has given us the papacy. Let us enjoy it!'" quoted the lady with the rings. "Isn't that what your brother Pope Leo said about it, Signora Salviati?" she asked Lucrezia with a false smile.

"As we are meant to enjoy all of God's gifts, Signora Farnese," Lucrezia countered sharply, with the same sort of smile, and then deftly steered the conversation in another direction.

It was urgent now that I talk with Ippolito before we were driven apart forever. At the end of April, just after I observed my twelfth birthday and Ippolito his twenty-second, I made up my mind to speak to him face-to-face, no matter how risky or difficult. I made certain that Alessandro was absent; I couldn't have borne his jeers and scathing remarks. I didn't care if anyone else saw me with Ippolito. What shame could be harder to bear, what punishment worse than the one I had already received?

After my tutors had gone for the day, I sat down on a bench outside the entrance to Ippolito's apartment, determined to stay there as long as it took. I hadn't long to wait before Ippolito emerged. He was splendidly dressed, and he'd grown a dark beard that made him even more handsome. I rose to greet him.

"Duchessina!" he exclaimed. "What are you doing here?"

"Waiting to speak to you, Ippolito. Is that not obvious?"

"But you shouldn't—"

"Never mind what I should or should not do!" I said, my voice quivering, although I had resolved not to break down weeping. "Come with me to the library. No one will know. Alessandro is gone—I saw him ride off."

Ippolito hesitated. "The Holy Father expects me."

"Let him wait!" I said sharply. "Surely you can find an excuse this one time!"

Ippolito's serious face broke into a smile. "I hadn't realized that you were so willful, Duchessina."

But my willfulness, if that's what it was, was of little use to me when we reached the library and shut the door behind us. "So," I began, before my decorum deserted me, "you will soon be a cardinal."

"It's not my choice, you must know that," Ippolito replied. He stood behind the table where we'd often sat side by side to study the drawings of the elephant and exchange words meant only for each other. Now the table was a barrier between us. "The Holy Father has determined this, and my protests mean nothing to him. I have no calling to the religious life—none! I've told him this, but he doesn't care to hear. You well know that Pope Clement holds all earthly power over our lives. And you must also know how deeply I care for you, Duchessina," he added softly.

"And I for you, Ippolito."

"If I had my choice, at the proper time I would have asked for your hand in marriage," he said. "It would have given me the greatest joy."

I gazed at him with a mixture of rapture and grief.

"But I would have been refused," he said. "The pope is your guardian, and he has grand plans for you. He's not going to waste one Medici on another—he has said as much. And so, to make sure we don't scheme to be together, he's made me a cardinal, soon to be sent away. I don't yet know where, but likely to some foreign country as a papal envoy. And you—" Ippolito hesitated. "Has Clement not yet spoken to you of this?"

I shook my head.

He sighed. "I've already gone too far, said too much. As Alessandro told you the last time we were here, you've had a number of suitors. The most powerful families in all of Europe are competing to provide you with a husband. The English ambassador has met several times with the pope to discuss the possibility of your marriage to the English King Henry VIII's bastard son, the Duke of Richmond. Another candidate is King James V of Scotland, although the pope believes England and Scotland are too far away to be considered."

"Can all this be true?" My legs felt so weak I had to lean on the table to keep from falling. "I care nothing for these prospective matches. I want *you*, Ippolito!"

"The pope is considering every possibility," Ippolito went on, "not in the light of what's best for *you* but what's best for *him*. Your future marriage is about Clement's political power, not your happiness. And certainly not mine."

I reached across the table toward my love, and he reached toward me. For one passionate moment that I knew I would never forget, our hands joined and we gazed into each other's eyes with longing.

"It cannot be, Duchessina," he whispered.

Ippolito let go of my hand, bowed deeply, and strode out of the library. The door closed behind him. I remained where I was, overwhelmed by feelings that didn't matter to anyone but myself. Then I flung myself down at the table and wept.

11

Alessandro

A TALL, THIN MAN with a long, mournful face arrived at Palazzo Medici carrying a sheaf of documents emblazoned with gilt seals. Sent by the new French ambassador to be my tutor in French, he was presented to me by Cardinal Giovanni.

"But why has the French ambassador sent me a tutor?" I asked the cardinal.

"His Holiness seeks to improve relations with France." The cardinal hesitated. "Perhaps you are to play a role in this improvement. A matter of diplomacy, you see."

"But what have I to do with it?"

"Perhaps it would be wise to wait and see," he advised.

The lessons began. His name was Monsieur Philippe, he told me with a bow that bent his narrow body nearly double. He spoke to me only in French. Slowly I began to understand and to respond, haltingly at first, and then with greater fluency.

Monsieur Philippe had a habit of appearing when and where I least expected him, unfashionably dressed in brown velvet with a flourish of lace at the ends of sleeves too short for his long arms. I might be out walking near the Piazza Navona with Maria and Francesca when Monsieur Philippe would pop out from behind a fountain or a tree and subject us all to a short discourse on botany, or architecture, or whatever else came to his mind—always in French, of course. This amused Maria but annoyed Francesca.

"He lacks manners," Francesca complained. "Like all the French."

Soon I could read and write in French as well. Monsieur Philippe was pleased.

"You learn quickly, *mademoiselle*," he said. "You grasp the grammar and the vocabulary with ease. But"—he lifted his shoulders in an unhappy shrug—"I fear that you will never speak our beautiful language with the proper accent. You must make a much greater effort with the pronunciation. Form your mouth like this"—he pursed his lips—"or no French person will understand what you are saying."

I did try, but the tutor's despair deepened. "Whatever you say always comes out sounding like Italian," he said sadly. "Endeavor to sound French, *mademoiselle, s'il vous plaît.*"

I still had not been told why, as "a matter of diplomacy," I was being required to learn the language, or for whose benefit I needed to sound French.

One day I asked Cornelius, my tutor in mathematics and astrology, to work out my horoscope. He had studied under the great philosopher-astrologer Marsilio Ficino of Florence, and I knew that the highest nobility of Rome consulted him for prognostications and guidance. "What does my future hold, *maestro*?" I asked. "I need to know."

Cornelius consulted the charts spread out on the library table and made numerous calculations, but the answer he finally presented was no answer at all: *You are destined to experience both great happiness and great sadness. There will be periods of power and of weakness, of success and of failure, of joy and grief. And you will have a long life.*

The first part was true: I had already enjoyed great happiness and endured sadness that nearly overwhelmed me. As to the rest of it, he claimed that the heavens revealed no more of what was in store for me.

Meanwhile, the pope likewise revealed no more of the life he was planning for me. Several times I made a formal request through Cardinal Giovanni or one of the other cardinals for a private audience with the Holy Father, but I was stalled—"His Holiness is a very busy man"—and finally refused outright. "His Holiness will summon you when he wishes to see you, *signorina*."

The summons did not come. I stopped asking.

———

THE WEEKS PASSED. Ippolito, who now wore the red hat of a cardinal, no longer had his quarters at Palazzo Medici. I saw him at dinners and other occasions to which Pope Clement invited me. These distant sightings seemed to taunt me. He was always surrounded by other churchmen. There was no chance to exchange even a formal greeting.

At the end of May the entire Salviati household moved to their handsome summer palace on a hill north of the city to escape the heat of the Roman summer. The villa was set among lovely gardens with cool breezes and sweeping views of the Tiber, the river that curled through the city like a silver ribbon. Musicians played at dinners served on the terrace after sunset. It was very pleasant, but my life felt like a huge empty drum. I yearned for Ippolito, sealed my unhappiness in a small chamber inside my heart, and waited for Destiny to show her hand.

When the Salviati household returned to the city at the end of summer, I realized that my efforts to avoid Alessandro might not be the best course of action. I was fairly certain that he knew what plans the pope had in store for me, as he'd seemed to know about candidates for my hand in marriage. Maybe rather than avoiding him, I should try to ingratiate myself instead.

I remembered lessons I'd learned when I was a child of six and Alessandro had called me "an ugly little thing." Although I was older now and filling out in the feminine places, I recognized that I would never be a beautiful woman. But I was also aware that I had developed a cer-

tain kind of attractiveness—some call it charm—and I
knew how to use that to my advantage. One didn't have to
like the person; one only had to be clever and pretend.
Much as I loathed Alessandro, I would beguile him and
bend him to my will.

I began my campaign with warm smiles and nods and
progressed to merry greetings: "*Buongiorno,* Alessandro!" I
sang out. "Good morning! I trust that all goes well with
you!" I bobbed a cheerful curtsy.

Then, swallowing my distaste, I suggested that we go
riding together. "I haven't enjoyed a brisk gallop for some
time," I told him. "And I value your lessons in horseman-
ship most highly. Perhaps you'd consent to an hour's ride
with the Frog Duchess?" I flashed a winsome smile.

"*Con piacere,* Duchessina," he replied. "With pleasure."

The unexpected invitation had the effect I wanted. He
was so used to taunting me and enjoying my angry and
sometimes tearful response that he seemed unsure what
to make of the change.

On a cool day toward the end of autumn, Alessandro
ordered the grooms to saddle our mounts. Soon we'd
crossed the Tiber, leaving the chaperoning ladies and
their servants far behind. Peasants in the fields looked up
as we galloped by in the warm autumn sunshine. We
reined our horses to a walk and turned back to look over
the city spread out below.

"What a magnificent city," I said with a heartfelt sigh,
glancing sidelong at Alessandro. "Although, truly, don't

you think Florence is more beautiful? I do miss the hills of Tuscany. And the Duomo! Surely it's the most glorious cathedral in all the world. I wonder," I mused aloud, "when the Holy Father will allow me to return there. Florence is the city of my birth, and I can't imagine spending my life anywhere else. Not even here in Rome." My horse nickered and tossed her head, impatient to be moving again, but I kept a firm grip on the reins. "And what about you, Alessandro?" I asked, smiling. "Do you look forward to going back to Florence?"

Alessandro's brow furrowed. He was even uglier when he frowned, but I kept the insincere smile firmly pasted on my face. "Certainly I do," he growled. "As Duke of Florence I will be lord over everyone. I'm to have a rich wife, the daughter of Emperor Charles. And I'll be living in Palazzo Medici—your former home, Duchessina—and have as many country villas and servants and horses as I want." A spiteful grin crept across his surly features. "Everyone in the family sings the praises of *Il Magnifico,* as though old Lorenzo was more important than anyone, more important than the pope. But I mean to show them that I am far more magnificent than *Il Magnifico* ever was," he boasted. "His image will fade in comparison to mine."

Alessandro was enjoying himself. I strived to keep my composure. "I've no doubt you'll bring even greater glory to Florence than our illustrious ancestor did," I lied.

He eyed me coolly. "And you, dear Duchessina?" he

said scornfully, his lip curled in a sneer. "You, too, are destined for greatness, are you not?"

I heard echoes of his past cruel taunts and felt my will crumbling. I wanted to lash out at him, to throw in his face that Pope Leo had always intended not him but Ippolito to rule Florence, and that he, Alessandro, was replacing Ippolito only because he was the pope's bastard son. *If Pope Leo were still alive,* I wanted to say, *it would be a different story altogether.*

I waited until I was sure of my next words. "I have no idea what lies ahead, cousin," I said carefully. Then I turned to him with my most engaging smile. "But perhaps *you* can tell *me?*"

"And what do I get in return, little Frog Duchess? Will you croak for me, if I tell you what I know?"

I checked a surge of anger at the mockery and made my voice soft and cajoling. "Alessandro, *per favore,* I beg you. We should not be enemies," I said, although I knew that wasn't true: We would always be enemies.

He stroked his straggly little beard, keeping me in suspense. "All right," he said at last. "I'll tell you what I know, just for the sheer pleasure of watching your face. Come, let's return to the city."

We started our horses at a sedate walk. "The French cardinal, Gramont—you met him last spring at the pope's dinner—was sent here to begin private conversations with His Holiness on behalf of the king of France,"

Alessandro said. "In the spring King François and Pope Clement signed a secret agreement."

Alessandro watched me. He enjoyed drawing out his story, observing my anxiety. "François is to receive title to several major cities under the pope's control: Pisa, Livorno, Parma, and others. And the pope promised to help François wrest Milan and Genoa away from Emperor Charles."

"But what has any of this to do with *me*?" I cried, my impatience growing.

"Everything. Their secret agreement is a marriage contract, dear Frog Duchess. These cities make up a part of your dowry. When you marry, they become the property of your husband, the lucky devil!"

"My dowry?" I nearly shouted. "But whom am I to marry? Tell me, Alessandro! Tell me, damn you!"

I had lost control, and I immediately regretted it. Now Alessandro held the advantage, and I had handed it to him. He knew he could torment me, make me beg.

His lips twisted in a derisive smile. "You are to be the bride of Henri, Duke of Orléans, second son of King François. Our Duchessina is to marry the brother of the future king of France! Just think of it—a French prince!"

With those words Alessandro whipped his stallion into a mad gallop. I urged my little mare to follow. She was smaller but very brave, and we managed to catch up with him before he thundered across the bridge. He reined in his horse and waited, laughing cruelly. "What is it, Duchessina? Haven't you heard enough?"

I was breathless and trembling, clutching the pommel. "There must be more. I'm sure you know more, Alessandro—tell me!"

Alessandro pulled on his lip, as though deep in thought. "Perhaps this will amuse you, then. King François requests that you come to live at the French court until you're of an age to wed." He looked me up and down in the insulting way I'd seen him eyeing the servant girls. "Anyone can see that you're not yet woman enough for marriage."

Not yet woman enough for marriage! I badly wanted to slap his ugly face. But it would not do to lose control again. I needed to hear the rest of his story.

His horse was dancing in nervous circles. Alessandro brought the stallion's head close to my mare's and thrust his own face close to mine. "The Holy Father refused that demand. His precious Duchessina is to remain under my loving care in Florence until the wedding."

"*Your* care, Alessandro?" Surely not! It couldn't be!

"Indeed. I'll let you know when we're leaving Rome."

I HAD TO SPEAK to Ippolito one more time. I had to tell him myself about the future that lay in store for me. But how was I to accomplish that? I wasn't permitted to go about in the streets of Rome without the company of at least one older woman, although I was certain I could convince Betta to go with me for a secret meeting. But where? When? And how to arrange it?

Then nothing short of a miracle happened: Monsieur Philippe brought me a letter. "I was walking near the river, as is my pleasure," the Frenchman reported in his doleful voice, "and a young boy asked me to bring this to you. A servant to one of the cardinals, I think."

I thought I recognized Ippolito's writing. I could scarcely wait for Monsieur Philippe to leave so that I could read it. The lesson in French subjunctives seemed endless.

At last I was alone. "Visit the chapel in the church of Santa Maria in Trastevere tomorrow at midafternoon," I read. "Seek out a monk at prayer. Do not reply to this message."

I read the letter over several times. I was sure the monk would turn out to be Ippolito himself. Why did he want to see me? Had something changed? Maybe he had told the pope that he did not want to be a cardinal, that he had no vocation in the church. Maybe—and here my imagination took flight—he'd even told the Holy Father that he loved me, his Duchessina, and he wanted to marry me. Maybe he was even making plans to go away with me. In my excitement I pushed the French prince and the marriage contract far from my mind.

"I must see him, and you must come with me," I insisted to Betta. "You understand, don't you?"

"I understand that your uncle the pope would send me away if he found out," she grumbled. But I knew her grumbling was only an act. Betta would give in and agree to do as I asked.

And she did. With each passing hour my conviction grew that my meeting with the "monk" would be a joyous one.

A cold rain had begun to fall. Wrapped in warm cloaks, Betta and I set off on foot. We crossed the Tiber and made our way through the narrow, crooked streets, unpaved and muddy. Soon our boots were caked with mud and our cloaks wet and splattered.

We entered the church, glad to be out of the rain. The sanctuary was dim and silent; a few old women, veiled in black, hovered near the altar, fingering their beads. We hurried past the chancel, where mosaics glowed in the light of dozens of flickering candles. The chapel was nearly empty, except for a monk in a rough woolen robe kneeling before the statue of the Blessed Virgin.

Betta nodded and retired to the rear of the chapel, and I approached the monk, eager to be with Ippolito but suddenly uneasy about whatever had led him to summon me there. *What if I'm wrong?* My knees were trembling as I knelt beside him. The monk turned toward me, pulling back his cowl to reveal his face.

It was not Ippolito.

"Alessandro!" I cried, shattering the silence.

He hushed me. "Are you disappointed, little Frog Duchess? Sad that your beloved Cardinal Ippolito couldn't come to you? He sent me in his place, with his profound apologies."

"I don't believe you," I said angrily. "Everything you say to me is a lie!"

"Duchessina, Duchessina!" Alessandro drawled, shaking his head. "You're being very childish. Ippolito left this morning for Hungary, where he's to serve as papal legate. Our cousin asked me to tell you how happy he is to learn of your coming marriage and wishes you great joy. I promised him I'd take good care of you in Florence."

Nearly ill with disappointment, I staggered clumsily to my feet. I could hardly speak. "Couldn't you have given me the same message at Palazzo Medici?" I stammered. "Why are you dressed like a monk? Why do you go to so much trouble to torment me?"

"Because it amuses me," said Alessandro. "You should also know that Cardinal Ippolito was quite eager to leave for his new assignment. Pope Clement has made it well worth his while, assigning him so many rich benefices that he couldn't refuse."

I glared at him in disgust. "Are you saying that the pope bribed him?"

"I'm saying that His Holiness offered Ippolito the income from a great deal of church property, and our cousin willingly accepted the pope's terms. Call that what you want." Alessandro rose and raised the cowl of the monk's robe. "I've delivered the message I was asked to give you. Now, with your permission, Duchessina, I leave you to your prayers to the Blessed Virgin."

He made his usual scornful bow and strode out of the chapel, and I sank to the stone floor. Betta knelt and wrapped her arms around me and rocked me like an infant as I wept.

IPPOLITO WAS GONE, without even a chance to say one last good-bye. Francesca, cheerful at last, had packed up her trousseau—and it was considerable—and left for Florence for her wedding to Ottavio de' Medici, accompanied by Lucrezia and Maria. Without Lucrezia, Pope Clement had no official hostess, and the number of dinners to which I was invited dwindled to nothing. This suited me very well.

I spent my days alone or with my tutors and buried myself in my studies. I made rapid strides in all my courses. Knowing now that I would one day live in France, I threw myself into the new language with as much energy as I could muster. I questioned Monsieur Philippe relentlessly about France and anything to do with the royal family.

"François, the Most Christian King, is the greatest ruler in all Europe," the tutor declared proudly. "Queen

Claude was loved by all before her death. She presented her husband the king with a child nearly every year, as was her duty. There are five children, three sons and two daughters. The new queen, Eleanor, is the most admirable of women."

"The names of the children, *s'il vous plaît*?" I prepared to write them down.

"François, the eldest who will one day be king, then Henri, followed by Madeleine, Charles, and Marguerite."

Henri, my future husband, interested me most, of course: *What is he like? How old is he? Is he handsome, intelligent, kind, like Ippolito? Or like Alessandro—ugly, badly spoiled, cruel?* But these weren't questions suitable to ask Monsieur Philippe, who presumably knew nothing of the secret agreement between the pope and the king.

"Are there many royal *palazzi*?" I asked, settling for a less difficult question.

"We call them *châteaux, mademoiselle,* and the answer is certainly," he replied. "Fontainebleau is the king's favorite. Also Amboise, Blois, Chambord, and many others as well. But why these questions, *mademoiselle*?"

"I may have occasion to travel to France some day soon. To visit the king," I added.

"Ahh," he replied, nodding. "I understand. Then undoubtedly you will see the *châteaux* for yourself."

Still I wasn't satisfied. "What sort of music does the king enjoy? What does the royal family eat? I've grown so accustomed to the ways of the papal court that I'm afraid I won't know what to do," I explained.

"Do not worry, *mademoiselle*," said Monsieur Philippe, stroking his long nose. "If you will just learn to speak the language beautifully, with the proper accent, I assure you that you will learn everything in good time."

⁂

MY COMING MARRIAGE was announced in January of 1533. But instead of Pope Clement himself telling me the news or sending me word through Cardinal Giovanni, I received a visit from the new French ambassador to Rome, John Stuart, Duke of Albany.

The ambassador turned out to be a relative by marriage—my uncle on my mother's side. Born in Scotland but raised in France, the duke had married my mother's sister. I had never known my aunt, Anne d'Auvergne; she'd died when I was a small child. Now her husband, the ambassador, called on me at Palazzo Medici to make a brief formal statement surrounded by a lot of flowery language: *Caterina de' Medici is to wed Henri, Duke of Orléans.*

I liked the ambassador at once. A stocky man with white streaks in his ruddy brown hair and beard, Albany lacked the elegance of the Frenchman who had once rescued me from the convent of Santa Lucia, but I felt that perhaps at last I had an ally. I plied him with questions.

"When am I to be married?" I asked.

"In October, Mademoiselle Catherine," he said, calling me by my French name.

"Why was my betrothal kept secret?"

"Allow me to explain a few things, *mademoiselle*. Pope Clement wanted to keep his agreement with King François a secret from Emperor Charles. Those two rulers have been enemies for many years. The Holy Father feared that if Charles learned of the agreement too soon, he would put a stop to the marriage contract. Now it's too late; there's nothing Charles can do about it. You're a most desirable bride—one of the richest women in Europe. The pope will not let you go cheaply."

But I had other things on my mind. *What about Henri?*— that's what mattered. *Will I like him? Will he care for me?*

But I couldn't bring myself to ask this honest-seeming ambassador. I would have to discover that for myself.

A NEW FACE appeared among the familiar ones at Palazzo Medici. It belonged to a distant Medici cousin called Lorenzino. Eighteen years old, nearly as handsome as Ippolito, and nearly as cruel and arrogant as Alessandro, Lorenzino quickly became Alessandro's constant companion in mischief. The pair soon brought down the wrath of Pope Clement for their malicious pranks, which included knocking the heads off antique statuary. Anyone could see that Lorenzino meant trouble, but the trouble was tolerated.

Pope Clement now announced that Alessandro would return to Florence to assume his new role as duke and lord over the city. Lorenzino, his loutish companion, would stand ready to help him. And I would accompany them both to the seat of Medici family power, to serve as Alessandro's official hostess and to prepare for my wedding.

When Lucrezia and Maria returned to Rome from Francesca's wedding, they were as surprised as anyone to learn of the marriage plans Pope Clement had made for me. Once again I would be separated from people I'd come to care for, especially Maria. Now they helped me get ready to leave Rome.

Lucrezia offered practical advice. "You're going to be expected to entertain a lot of people at a lot of dinners. Hire the best cooks you can find and pay them well, keep an eye on the budget, fire anyone you suspect of cheating you, and smile at your guests no matter how terrible you feel. Act as though you know exactly what you're doing. I'm sure you'll be a brilliant hostess." I hoped she was right.

At the end of January, His Holiness arranged a farewell dinner for me. Maria laughed as she arranged my hair, recalling the stubble I'd arrived with, but our laughter turned to weeping before she'd finished. We left Palazzo Medici with Lucrezia to ride together to the pope's residence for the last time.

Pope Clement's tears flowed as freely as they had two years earlier when I'd first arrived in Rome. "I've made the greatest match in the world for you, dear niece," he whispered as I knelt and kissed his ring.

"*Mille grazie,* Holy Father," I replied softly. "I am most grateful."

On a cold February day I embraced Lucrezia and Maria and rode out of the Eternal City with Alessandro's huge retinue headed north, thinking of all that I was leaving behind and all that lay ahead.

12

Preparing for Marriage

WHEN BETTA AND I arrived in Florence with Alessandro's entourage, we found the Palazzo Medici in a sorry state of disrepair, with the furnishings stolen or vandalized during the siege. Alessandro angrily dismissed the trusted servant who had been left in charge of the palazzo and ordered the flogging of the slaves under his direction.

Dismayed, I laid a hand on his arm and tried to restrain him. "Surely it's not their fault," I ventured. "The mobs—"

"Who are you to tell me what to do?" Alessandro interrupted rudely, shaking me off.

Soon he'd installed a new staff, including a Turkish slave girl to attend to my personal needs. Her name was

Akasma. She had been brought from Constantinople with her mother, who had died on the voyage, and put in a group of slaves bought by Alessandro. At fifteen she was only a year older than I but a dozen years wiser. She was very tall, exotically beautiful with high cheekbones and almond-shaped eyes, graceful and intelligent. She had a fine singing voice the choir nuns at Le Murate would have welcomed, but she hadn't been trained in the virtues and had a worrisome way of meeting a man's stares.

I hadn't been around girls my own age since I'd left Le Murate more than two years earlier. In Akasma I found someone who could be a friend, in spite of our social differences, and I quickly became attached to her. I invented excuses to have her come to my apartment on some trivial errand. Sometimes she talked her way into the servants' kitchen late in the evening and prepared an orange-flavored pudding, which we then shared.

Akasma was thrilled to learn that I would soon travel to France to be married. I was determined to take her with me, an idea that appealed to her adventurous spirit.

"Tell me about France," she begged.

"No doubt we'll live in huge castles even grander than this one, and we'll be well cared for by the king of France himself." Beyond that, I had no more idea than she did what to expect.

"And Alessandro—will he come to the wedding, too?"

"I don't know. Why do you ask?"

She shrugged. "I don't like him."

"Oh, Akasma," I said. "Nobody does."

WITHIN A WEEK of my return to Florence, I arranged to visit Le Murate. I went first to see the abbess, Suor Margherita, who assured me that all was well—the gardens had been restored to their earlier beauty, the nuns were again plump and in good health, and loyal patrons had placed orders for bridal trousseaux and for copies of the Book of Hours.

I asked about my dear friends. "Are they still here?"

"Niccolà and Giulietta are waiting for the next stage in their lives to begin, when dowry negotiations are complete," the abbess reported. "And Tomassa weeps constantly, still fearing that her father hasn't enough dowry to find her a suitable husband and that she will have to spend the rest of her life as a nun."

"I want to invite them to travel with me to France for my wedding," I told her.

"Go speak to them. I'll grant them leave for the journey, if their parents are agreeable."

The rules had not changed: Visits were still limited to a few minutes at the grille, with no chance to speak face-to-face.

"Oh, Duchessina, it's you!" I recognized Niccolà's voice. "We've missed you! Tell us everything!"

This was the first time I had stood on the outside of the grille to visit someone on the inside. It was better than nothing, I thought, but unsatisfying when there was so much more to say. "You know I have only minutes here. But I want to ask you—all three of you—to my wedding. I'm to marry Henri, Duke of Orléans, second son of the king of France. Will you join my retinue and make the journey to France?"

Such excitement! Of course they would. "If our parents allow it," Tomassa added.

"I'll write to them," I promised.

Suor Margherita signaled the end of the visit. "Come back soon, Duchessina!" they called after me.

BEFORE I LEFT ROME, the Duke of Albany had promised to send me a dancing master to teach me to dance in the French manner. Now a short, round man with a small black mustache and dainty white hands appeared at Palazzo Medici. "Monsieur Sagnier, master of the dance, at your service, *mademoiselle.*"

I remembered the nights in the convent when Argentina boldly organized secret dancing parties while the nuns slept. Under Monsieur Sagnier's instruction I learned that, with slight differences, the French dances were much the same—the slow *basse danse,* the stately *pavane.* Next he added the *gaillarde,* full of leaps and hops. Akasma was drafted to serve as my partner.

When the day's lesson ended, I plied Monsieur Sagnier with questions. Unlike Monsieur Philippe or the Duke of Albany, the dancing teacher was a willing source of gossip.

"King François loves women—especially beautiful women," Monsieur Sagnier told me, little black mustache twitching. "His favorite is Anne d'Heilly, his mistress. Then there is Queen Eleanor, who is not beautiful and whom he loves not at all."

I gaped at Monsieur Sagnier, considering this bit of information, which didn't match what the French tutor had told me. I sometimes felt that the dancing master embroidered his stories. How, for instance, could it possibly be true what he now claimed had happened to Henri and his older brother?

"The king of France and the king of Spain had long been arch rivals," he explained. "François wanted to be Holy Roman Emperor, but the electors chose Charles instead. One can scarcely imagine the battles that followed, the wars, the hostility between the two kings!" Sagnier's pale fingers fluttered.

"Then Charles defeated François and took him prisoner, locking him up in a Spanish prison. The next year the two kings made their peace, but to earn his freedom François had to agree to marry Charles's widowed sister, Eleanor, the one he does not love, and to hand over his two older sons as hostages. The dauphin was eight and Henri just six years old when they were sent away to a harsh prison in Spain."

"His own sons?" I repeated, incredulous. "King François bought his own freedom by giving the Spanish his two boys as hostages?" I wondered if I had misunderstood—that my comprehension of French was not as good as I thought.

"*Oui, exactement.* The boys remained for four years in a miserable dungeon, until their release was finally arranged."

"How terrible!" I cried. My months at Santa Lucia had taught me what it was to be a hostage, but my future husband's childhood had been much worse than mine. Maybe we shared a common bond after all.

WORK BEGAN IMMEDIATELY on wedding preparations. According to the marriage contract, Pope Clement was to provide me with an enormous trousseau, requiring not just one large *cassone* but several. So many Florentine makers of *cassoni* had died in the siege that the carved and painted wooden chests had to be ordered from the finest craftsmen in the town of Lucca.

There was also a shortage of fine fabrics as well as a lack of expert seamstresses to sew and embroider my gowns. To solve these problems, the pope enlisted the help of his friend, Isabella d'Este, Duchess of Mantua, a woman greatly admired for her exquisite taste. She immediately began sending from Mantua quantities of gold and silver tissue and the finest silk brocade for my gowns.

Heavy black, crimson, and gold damask were ordered for bedcoverings and curtains. Sheer linen was sent for my sleeping shifts and underthings.

Bolts of cloth began to arrive at the palazzo, along with quantities of lace and bobbins of gold thread. Casks of tiny pearls, amethysts, opals, garnets, rubies, emeralds, topaz, and sapphires were delivered under guard. Seamstresses came to take my measurements and study the sketches sent by the duchess, returning days later with half-finished gowns and petticoats to be tried on, fitted, and taken back to workrooms for final stitching before being sent on to the embroiderers. Soon my trousseau occupied an entire room of my apartment.

I WISHED TO AVOID Alessandro, but that proved impossible. He expected me to act as his official hostess. Night after night the elite of Florentine society—and some of Alessandro's not so elite friends—swarmed the refurbished reception hall, newly plastered and hung with rich tapestries that I'd selected. Servants raced up and down from the kitchen to serve the guests with food and drink that I'd ordered. Musicians I'd hired provided music, and the talk grew louder and the laughter more raucous as the wine flowed freely. Dressed in one of my new gowns of rustling taffeta or sensuous velvet, cut low in front to show off my newly developed breasts and the jewels that hung just above them, I passed long hours smiling and chatting with the bankers and merchants still loyal to the house of Medici. I followed Aunt Lucrezia's advice, and it seemed to work.

Among the frequent guests was Filippo Strozzi. One night he drank more than usual and consequently talked more, too. He congratulated me on my coming marriage and then let it slip that he had loaned Pope Clement a considerable sum of money for my wedding: "More than one hundred thirty thousand ducats," he confided.

"A very large sum, Uncle," I murmured.

"You're taking with you to France a dowry fit for a queen! But it's a sound investment for the Strozzi bank. His Holiness guaranteed the loan with a gold and diamond brooch and other jewels from the Vatican treasury."

A dowry fit for a queen, I mused as I moved on to greet a new arrival. *For me!* It still seemed hard to believe.

Most of the evenings ended with Alessandro and Lorenzino staggering drunkenly out the door with their equally drunken friends. After the last of the guests had gone, I climbed wearily to my apartment and often fell on my bed fully clothed, letting Akasma undress me and cover me with an embroidered sheet to sleep as long as I could.

I had been back in the Palazzo Medici of Florence barely two months when Alessandro assigned me another duty: hostess to Margaret of Austria, the emperor's daughter and Alessandro's future bride. Margaret was traveling to Naples from her home in the Netherlands and planned to spend several days resting in Florence.

Remembering the graciousness with which Lucrezia always welcomed guests to her palace in Rome, I made up my mind to do my best for this girl.

Accompanied by Akasma and my usual guards, I rode out to greet her on the road from the north. It was a shining April day just after my fourteenth birthday. We had arranged to meet in a pretty valley where spring flowers bloomed in profusion. In spite of my weariness from my many duties, I enjoyed getting out into the countryside. I felt pity for any unfortunate girl who would marry Alessandro, but when I saw what a sweet and intelligent little thing she was, my heart nearly broke for her.

Margaret had gathered a nosegay of lilies of the valley and presented them to me when we met. She was just ten years old, and I was sure this innocent child had no idea that when she came of age she was to marry a monster whose depravity was as well known in Florence as it was in Rome.

Margaret stayed at Palazzo Medici, and I did what I could to keep her away from Alessandro after the obligatory meeting and a dinner arranged in her honor. Alessandro showed not the slightest interest in his future bride, who sat beside me at the dinner. I saw her glancing at him with a puzzled look, but she asked no questions. Alessandro ended the dinner early and left with Lorenzino. That was the last we saw of him. He was much too busy debauching himself with the loose women of the city to bother with a ten-year-old girl.

Together Margaret and I visited the Duomo, the largest cathedral in Europe, gazed at the Campanile and the bronze doors of the baptistery and Michelangelo's sculpture of David with its damaged arm, both of us sneaking curious glances at his nakedness and pretending not to. Our best moments were spent quietly in the Chapel of the Magi, surrounded by the frescoes I loved.

After three days I rode with her to the city walls and kissed her and wished her well. *Thank God there will be no wedding for at least four years,* I thought. *Anything could happen. For her sake, I pray that it will!*

EARLY IN MAY, Alessandro came unannounced to my apartment while Akasma was fixing my hair. It had grown long enough so that I'd been spending hours on the roof wearing a special sun hat to protect my complexion while allowing my hair to bleach to a lighter shade, which was the latest fashion. We were preparing for the arrival of Giorgio Vasari, Alessandro's artist friend who'd been commissioned to paint my portrait as a gift for the French king.

Alessandro carried a medal at the end of a chain. He'd had a series of medals cast with his profile from the remains of La Vacca, the bell that had once symbolized the city's freedom. He twirled it around his finger, this way and that, while he stared boldly at Akasma.

"You're awaiting Vasari? Don't worry, dear cousin," he

said in the sardonic tone that so angered me. "I've asked my friend to paint you as you'd want your future husband to see you—not as the little Frog Duchess," he said. He smirked and continued to leer at Akasma.

Akasma ignored him. She always seemed tense when he was around. While she worked a garland of small jewels into my hair, Akasma started humming one of my favorite songs, about a twining rose and a rippling stream. She began softly enough, but soon she was singing in a scratchy, off-key voice, louder and louder. It was painful to hear. Alessandro stared at her for a moment before he fled from the room, hands over his ears to shut out the dreadful squawks.

Akasma and I glanced at each other in the mirror and started laughing. "So you see," said the slave, "I know how to get rid of a troublesome fellow."

"But you can't always be singing," I pointed out, worrying what could happen to her, now that he'd taken notice of her. "And he can order you to be silent."

Akasma shrugged. "I know—I'm a slave, and he'll do as he wants with me. But I'll do what I can, for as long as I can."

WORK BEGAN ON the portrait. Each time Giorgio Vasari came, Betta settled in as chaperone and Akasma stood by, ready to bring me a cup of watered wine when I asked for it.

I liked Vasari and wondered how this fine artist and

good-tempered man could have become Alessandro's friend. All of his friends were bullies, I thought—arrogant, cruel, somewhat stupid. Vasari was none of these. He talked to me as he worked. He was so kind, so amusing, that I tried hard to please him, holding the pose for long periods without asking for a rest.

But it was Giorgio Vasari who needed the rests, sometimes simply going into the next room to sit with his eyes closed. Once he went out to dine with Alessandro, promising to return later. As soon as he'd gone, I stepped around to the front of the painting to see what he had made of my features. Alessandro was right—Giorgio hadn't portrayed me as a Frog Duchess, but neither had he shown me as the beauty that I wished to be. My eyes were still too large and prominent, my cheeks too round, my chin too small.

But changes could be made! I picked up one of the brushes, tipped it in a rosy hue, and gave the face in the portrait the bright coloring of the audacious women I'd seen around the old market. Akasma's mouth formed a shocked O when she saw what I'd done, and I'd barely had time to lay aside the brush when the artist returned, refreshed and ready to paint again.

"Shall we resume, *signorina*?" he asked with his usual pleasant smile. "The portrait is nearly finished. We'll have a fine likeness to send off to the king of France. I confess, Signorina Duchessina, I regret that we are finished. I have delighted in your company, and I trust that I may again have the honor of attempting to capture on canvas the charm and wit of such a gracious subject."

I merely smiled and resumed my pose.

Giorgio stepped behind his easel. At first his face went quite white, and then quite red. "*La duchessina* is dissatisfied with my work?" he asked cautiously. "She would perhaps like some adjustments made to her portrait?"

I couldn't restrain my laughter. "I meant nothing by it, Signor Vasari," I explained. "I was just having a little amusement."

Vasari startled me by dropping to his knees at my feet. "My dear *signorina*," he said, hands clasped over his heart. "Were it possible, were you not so far above me in your station in life, and were you not soon to marry into the French royal family, I swear that I would declare my love for you and pledge my eternal devotion."

It was my turn to blush, and I thanked him for his kind sentiments. I truly regretted the moment when he announced that the portrait was finished, kissed my hand, and said good-bye.

FOR DAYS AFTER the tuneless singing incident, I worried about Akasma. I remembered the hungry, lascivious look on Alessandro's face as he watched her, and I should have known what was coming. She couldn't keep singing off-key forever. One day she confessed to me that he had forced himself upon her, trapping her when she was washing my linens.

"I'm safe only when I'm here with you," she told me, and for the first time I saw tears glittering in her eyes. "Now he comes to me at night in the servants' quarters and doesn't care who sees him or knows what he's about. And his cousin, Lorenzino—I'm afraid of him, too."

"Why didn't you tell me this before?" I demanded. "You must stay with me from now on."

That very day we arranged to have her few belongings brought to my apartment. She would sleep on a pallet beside my bed.

"Now you'll be safe," I assured her. "And I've learned that Alessandro has decided to move to the Palazzo dei Signoria. He says it's better fortified in the event of an uprising."

This was good news, but until he was gone, I hadn't worked out how she could avoid encountering Alessandro as she went about her duties. He regularly rampaged through the household, ordering slaves to be whipped when they didn't obey his orders quickly enough, striking fear in the hearts of everyone who lived there. Lorenzino, too, skulked around like a cheetah about to pounce.

"Within a few months we'll be on our way to France," I promised my slave, "and you'll no longer need to worry about those two."

I tried to reassure her and myself, but we both knew

that, although she served me, she belonged to Alessandro. I decided to ask him to give her to me as a wedding gift. If he refused, I would offer to buy her. Surely he had no reason to object. I needed her wit and wisdom, for she had a way of seeing the world with a clarity that I hadn't yet acquired. And I needed her friendship.

But everything depended on Alessandro.

FOR WEEKS, every communication that arrived from Pope Clement trumpeted that this wedding, this union of two great families of Europe, was to be the grandest celebration of the century. It would take place in October in Marseilles. I must be ready to leave Florence on the first of September—less than three months away. My uneasiness, mild at first, began to increase.

I visited Le Murate again to tell my friends that their parents had all agreed to the journey. Their excitement and enthusiasm helped to ease my mind.

But I still had not spoken to Alessandro about Akasma. I was afraid that if he knew how much I wanted her, he would find a way to use that to bargain. I was waiting for the right moment, but one day when I saw him alone in the garden, I decided that the "right" moment might never come. I made up my mind to approach him.

"I want to take Akasma with me to France," I said simply. "Will you give her to me as a wedding gift?"

He studied my face, probably trying to determine how

badly I wanted her. I kept my face as blank as I could, revealing nothing.

"Perhaps," he said. "I'll think about it."

"*Grazie*," I said, and walked away. *The devil take you if you decide against it, Alessandro!*

AT THE BEGINNING of the summer our household moved to Poggio a Caiano, where the weather was cooler and occasional showers freshened the vineyards and olive groves. Seamstresses and embroiderers and furriers and jewelers set up workshops there and continued to enlarge my trousseau. I was occupied from sunrise to sunset with fittings and countless details. Sleeves longer or shorter? Blue ribbons or white? *Will this never end?* I wondered wearily.

Because I was small and I'd heard that my bridegroom and his father and brothers were all quite tall, I ordered special footwear from Venice, chopines with thick platform soles that added several inches to my height. Chopines made walking difficult, but I practiced every day so that I wouldn't trip or turn my ankle. I learned to perform deep curtsies without toppling over. But I realized that trouble would come if I tried to dance in them.

"I have an idea," Akasma said after she'd watched me totter around. "Keep the sole high in back, beneath the heel, and have it cut down low in front, under your toes. Then you'll still be taller, but you'll walk more easily. Maybe you can dance, too."

I summoned a local cobbler immediately and explained Akasma's idea. He was skeptical, but two days later he returned with a pair of shoes that were high in back, low in front. I tried them on and began walking in them. Soon I was dancing without wobbling.

"Perfect!" I cried. "Now make me a dozen pairs!"

We entertained visitors from the city—Niccolà and Giulietta and Tomassa and their families came for a week. The widow, Maria Salviati, visiting from Rome, brought her sister, Francesca, and Francesca's new husband, Ottavio de' Medici, for an extended stay. At dinner we discussed arrangements for the journey to France. Betta clucked and hovered, overseeing the packing with help from Akasma. The days passed too quickly. There was still too much to do. I was tired. My temper was short, and my uneasiness increased.

Whenever we could manage to escape, Akasma and I ran down to the riverbank, where we lolled in the tall grass and talked. Here I finally gathered my courage and whispered my greatest fears to her: I had no idea what to expect on my wedding night. There had been no woman in the family to instruct me in these mysteries. I might have expected Maria Salviati, or even the elderly Lucrezia, to offer some enlightenment, but they had not.

Nor had Betta, who'd explained to me what was happening when my body changed from a girl's to a woman's. "Now you're ready to beget children," Betta had told me, "the joy and the duty of every woman." But when

I had asked how the begetting came about, she brushed aside my question. "Time enough for you to learn about that business when you're married. Don't worry—your husband will teach you whatever you need to know. As mine did me."

Now I turned to Akasma. Not yet sixteen, she seemed worldly and knowing about many things that I had no knowledge of. And, I knew, she had been initiated into the mysteries by Alessandro.

Akasma laughed at my questions. "How is it possible that you don't know even the simplest things? Have you never seen animals perform the act? It's not so different for humans."

I remembered a stallion I had once seen with a mare when I was out riding, and the crude remarks Alessandro had made. I had looked away then, not really understanding. Now I understood, and my stomach turned. "And that's how it will be for me?" I asked, my voice quivering.

"If you're fortunate, this French boy you're marrying will have had lots of experience before you turn up in his bed, and he will be kind to you. But whether he's kind or crude, there's not much you can do about it."

She went on to describe to me in plain language what was going to happen on my wedding night. When I shuddered, she offered this advice: "Remove your mind from the scene and think of something pleasant. Remember what it was like when we were here today—sweet-smelling flowers, warm sunshine, laughter. It will help you."

I thanked her for her advice and promised to follow it.

Akasma plucked a reed from the riverbank and chewed the stem thoughtfully. "Have you spoken to Alessandro? Will he allow me to go with you to France?"

"I asked him. He said he would let me know. I'm afraid to press him, because then he's sure to refuse."

Akasma sighed. "This is as good a time as any to tell you: Alessandro came after me again. When I tried to get away, he threatened to have me whipped if I didn't submit. 'I would rather be whipped,' I told him. I struggled, but the harder I fought, the more he laughed. In the end he overpowered me."

"The beast!" I cried. "Surely he must be punished for this!"

Akasma spat out the stem. "Punished by whom, Duchessina? He's the Duke of Florence and I'm a slave— I'm the one who will be punished, not Alessandro. That's the way of the world, and I must make the best of it."

I thought of Suor Immacolata, the nun at Santa Lucia who'd spoken of my father: *Lorenzo ruined me, and left me to bear his child.* Is that what had happened to Akasma? I studied her face. "Are you with child?" I asked, fearing the answer.

Akasma looked away. "Two months gone."

"Does Alessandro know?"

She shook her head.

"Then we must make sure he doesn't find out. You'll travel with me to France and bear your child there. All will be well."

All will be well. I'd believed that in the past, but it hadn't turned out that way. If Alessandro found out about the child, he would insist that it belonged to him—especially if it were a boy. I dared not press him; that practically guaranteed his refusal.

BY THE END OF AUGUST everything was ready. The time had come to leave Florence, perhaps forever. To my dismay, Alessandro announced his intention to travel with my entourage on the first stage of the journey to France. If he decided he wanted Akasma after all, it would be impossible to keep her safe from him. I had no idea how to protect her.

13

The Wedding

THE DAY BEFORE I began my journey to a new life, I entertained the wives and daughters of the leading noblemen of Florence at a dinner. Remembering the months when we'd all gone hungry, I ordered the cooks at Palazzo Medici to prepare a feast: roast capons and pigeons and quail, a whole suckling pig, several kinds of vegetables, ravioli stuffed with spinach, tortes made with eggs and cheese, bowls of nuts and olives, all to be served with the finest wines from Alessandro's cellar. The final presentation was an elaborate model of Venus and Cupid made of sugar, so amazingly lifelike that it drew gasps from the ladies. I knew they'd be talking about the dinner for weeks, and that pleased me.

The next morning I paced anxiously in my apartment

as Betta finished packing the *cassoni*, each wooden chest decorated with scenes from Greek mythology and now filled with part of my enormous trousseau. Akasma ran up and down the stairs, watching as the chests were strapped onto a specially built cart; panniers on the backs of pack animals carried the rest of our belongings. Once we reached La Spezia on the coast, we would board ships and sail to Marseilles; the baggage would go by an overland route, except for my little *cassone*. That I insisted on carrying with me.

In the crowd preparing to travel that day were Filippo and my Strozzi cousins, my three friends from Le Murate, Maria Salviati from Rome, and a large number of Medici relatives or people claiming to be relatives, many of whom I'd never met until that day—and all of them had their servants as well as governesses for the younger girls. The number was in the hundreds. King François had sent seventy gentlemen of the French court to provide an escort. At midafternoon the chief steward announced that everything was ready, and we must leave immediately in order to reach our first stop by nightfall.

I braced for my painful separation from Betta, who had decided to stay in Florence.

"I have no wish to see more of the world, Duchessina," she'd told me, "and I'm frightened of the sea voyage. Just making the journey to Rome was hard enough on these old bones. I'm an old woman, and I want to die here, in my own country."

"You're not an old woman!" I'd insisted when she first told me her decision in midsummer. Since then I had tried every argument I could think of, but I hadn't changed her mind. Now the time had come, and we clung to each other and wept.

"Akasma will see that you're well cared for," Betta said between sobs, although I don't think Betta believed anyone could possibly care for me as well as she had.

The steward came to separate us. "Signorina," he said, bowing to me, *"per favore."*

"God go with you, dear Duchessina!" cried Betta, as I climbed onto my mule. I watched her wave and wave until I lost sight of her.

The great procession wended its way across the Arno River on a bright, hot September afternoon like a huge beast, moving in fits and starts. I glanced back at the Duomo and wondered if I would ever see it again. I was both excited and anxious about what lay ahead for me. My head throbbed. My stomach churned.

Akasma was eager to be on our way, although she was troubled, as I was, that Alessandro had decided to accompany our retinue as far as Villefranche on the coast of France. He had elected not to continue on to Marseilles for the wedding but to return to Florence, fearing, I supposed, that he couldn't afford to be absent for more than a few weeks without trouble breaking out in the city he was determined to dominate.

The sun was setting as we neared Poggio a Caiano,

where we intended to pass the night, when out of a cloud of dust several horsemen appeared at full gallop. They identified themselves as emissaries from King François; they had taken a different road to Florence, discovered that we had already left, and ridden hard to catch up with us. The gentleman in charge leaped from his sweating horse and dropped to one knee beside my mule. "A welcoming gift from His Majesty, King François," he explained, and presented me with a magnificent diamond and sapphire pendant.

Akasma fastened the pendant around my neck. "A good sign," she whispered. The king's generous gesture made me feel a little calmer. *All will be well,* I told myself for perhaps the hundredth time.

AFTER FIVE DAYS we reached La Spezia on the Italian coast. I was enjoying my first sight of the sparkling waters of the Mediterranean when Alessandro drew up next to me. Akasma, who'd been walking beside my mule, slipped quietly away.

"Lovely view, isn't it, Duchessina?" asked Alessandro, his glance flickering idly after Akasma. I agreed that it was.

"It has occurred to me," he said, "that I haven't yet presented you with a wedding gift. And so I've brought with me something I believe you'll find invaluable in your new life." He handed me a book from his leather bag. "With my good wishes."

The book was well printed on rich parchment—Suor Battista would have scorned it, since it wasn't copied by hand—and elegantly bound. "*The Prince,* written by Niccolò Machiavelli," I read aloud. I held it for a moment. "I'm grateful, but this is not the gift I asked for. I've asked you for Akasma. I'll pay you whatever you ask, if only you'll agree to it."

"You'll have my answer in a few days, I promise you," he said. "Meanwhile, you can read the book. Machiavelli dedicated it to your father when the duke was first citizen of Florence and destined to follow in the footsteps of *Il Magnifico.* Study it carefully—it will tell you all you'll need to know to be an effective ruler. 'The end justifies the means for the good of the state,' for instance. You may want to keep that in mind."

"I'm grateful for the gift, dear cousin," I said. "It will be a fine addition to any library. But I have no use for the advice you've described. I'm not destined to rule."

The procession had started forward again. "Don't be foolish, Duchessina," Alessandro said. "You're bound to end up as queen of France one day—and don't pretend to be shocked! My sources tell me that the king's eldest son is sickly and unlikely to inherit the crown, or to wear it for long. That means your soon-to-be husband will be king and you will be his queen. After that, who knows what Fate has in store? Whether you're a Frog Duchess or a humble slave, it's best to be prepared—don't you agree?"

Something in his tone alerted me. "My slave," I said. "I need your answer, Alessandro. Don't disappoint me."

"You have nothing to fear, Duchessina," he replied. "It will be taken care of." He spurred his horse and trotted off.

THE DUKE OF ALBANY greeted me at the port city of La Spezia. He stood by with twenty-seven sailing ships to transport us to Villefranche.

What a thrilling time it was for me and for my ladies! I had never been on a ship. Before Giulietta even set foot on the deck, she declared that she was seasick. But our two days under sail on shimmering blue waters proved delightful, and we dropped anchor in a peaceful harbor ringed with green hills. There we would await the arrival of Pope Clement.

We found ways to amuse ourselves while we waited. Monsieur Philippe and Monsieur Sagnier traveled with us and provided French lessons and dancing classes to anyone interested. I strolled with my ladies along the waterfront of the little fishing village, always keeping watch for the arrival of the pope's ships. A month passed. Our initial excitement gave way to tedium and nerves. The Duke of Albany kept assuring us that the Holy Father was on his way.

At last the pope's fleet of some sixty vessels sailed into the harbor, led by a galley named *La Duchessina* in my honor, carrying the Holy Sacrament. A military escort followed, and last came the pope's own ship, *The Servant of*

God, built for this occasion. Dozens of fishing boats rowed out to greet it. Beneath the mainsail of purple silk embroidered with gold, three hundred rowers in red and yellow satin bent to their oars. Under a great purple awning sat Pope Clement VII on a throne draped in gold brocade. On shore crowds of peasants who'd flocked down from the hills for a glimpse of the Holy Father ate and drank and danced tirelessly until the sun rose the next day.

During the welcoming ceremonies—kissing the pope's ring, receiving his blessing—I watched Alessandro's familiar swagger, glad that shortly I would be seeing the last of him. But I was nearly knocked breathless when I sighted Ippolito among the dozens of cardinals traveling with the pope. He had come back from Hungary, then; what plans had the pope made for him now? Would he have a chance to tell me? I spent so much time gazing after him that Niccolà inquired who he might be.

"A cousin," I replied, and let it go at that.

After Mass had been celebrated and all the necessary ceremonies observed, the Duke of Albany signaled that our journey would continue. On the ninth of October we again boarded our ship. Akasma went to see that my things were properly accounted for, and my friends and I crowded the rail as the ships left the harbor. People on the shore grew smaller. I glanced around the deck, expecting Akasma to join me. I didn't see her. Perhaps she had gone below. *But she should be here, with me,* I thought.

I turned to Niccolà. "Have you seen Akasma?" I asked.

"Your slave? The Turkish girl? I believe I saw her with Alessandro."

"Alessandro! But he went ashore, didn't he?"

"I think so. And he had someone with him. A girl. Maybe a slave—I can't be sure," she said, her attention somewhere else. "There's so much happening, Duchessina! Isn't it marvelous?"

I ran from one person to another. "Have you seen Akasma, my Turkish slave?" I cried. "Very tall, almond eyed, beautiful?"

No one had. I rushed to the captain and borrowed his spyglass to scan the quickly receding shoreline.

"Perhaps she's run away," Niccolà suggested. But I guessed what had happened: Alessandro had abducted her. *You have nothing to fear,* he'd said. *It will be taken care of.* So this was how he had taken care of it! Hatred of Alessandro and fear for Akasma's fate drained my strength, and I sat down clumsily on the deck and buried my face in my hands. My ladies clustered around me worriedly. "Duchessina, what's wrong?" Giulietta asked. "Are you ill?"

I shook my head. *Heaven only knows what will happen to her,* I thought. *I'll never see her again.* "Just a slight weakness. It's nothing," I said, and allowed my friends to help me to my feet.

THE GREAT FLEET sailed into the harbor of Marseilles two days later. Cannons boomed from the ramparts surrounding the city, answered by salvos from the guns on our ships. Smoke and flames blackened the sky, and the noise was deafening. My ladies, at first elated by the commotion, now cowered near me. "It's like the siege, when our city was bombarded for weeks at a time," Giulietta said, choking back fearful sobs.

"There's nothing to be afraid of," I assured them, more bravely than I felt. "The Duke of Albany tells me this is meant to be a welcome."

Once the smoke had cleared, a flotilla of small boats surrounded our ships and rowed us all ashore. The clamor continued: Church bells pealed, trumpets and clarions blasted fanfares. And this was just the beginning.

Arrangements had been made for us to remain outside of Marseilles that night, giving me one last chance to have my servants search again for the missing Akasma. I had clung to the hope that she might have mistakenly boarded another ship. When they failed to find her, I wept into my pillow, vowing, *I will never forgive Alessandro for this.*

The next morning, Sunday, Pope Clement made his official entry into Marseilles, the procession led by a high-stepping white horse carrying the Holy Sacrament. Next came the Holy Father on his gilded throne, borne on the shoulders of a dozen Swiss Guards. The cardinals followed, riding two by two. Ippolito was among them, but he didn't look my way.

A day later King François made his formal entry with Queen Eleanor and the king's sons and daughters and members of the French court, accompanied by some five hundred soldiers, archers, and guards. Somewhere in that crowd was my future husband. I strained for a glimpse and tried to guess: *Which one is he?*

My official entry was not scheduled for another nine days, to allow time for the king and the pope to work out the final details of the marriage contract. It seemed very complicated, for it involved not only my dowry of gold and jewels but also control of several Italian cities now ruled by Emperor Charles. I understood that my marriage was the linchpin holding it all together.

Pope Clement and King François and their retinues were accommodated in two neighboring palaces with a bridge connecting them. While king and pope negotiated, the rest of us were free to amuse ourselves. The weather was still mild on the coast of France, much warmer than in Florence, where the autumn rains had no doubt begun to fall. Some of the gentlemen borrowed boats from local fishermen to take the ladies on picnics to the fine secluded beaches. My friends, enjoying their first whiffs of freedom, were determined to go on these outings, and if it hadn't been for the governesses sent along by the girls' parents, I would have had a hard time of it protecting their reputations and their virtue.

I was far too apprehensive to be tempted by these diversions. I still grieved over the disappearance of Akasma, who would have been able to soothe my fears and quiet the misgivings. Occasional glimpses of Ippolito allowed me to wonder if he might find a way to send me one last message, or even to speak to me one last time. If Akasma had been there, she would have carried secret messages; she would have had sensible advice.

And Akasma might have been able to find out something about Henri. I hadn't yet been presented to my future husband. I still wasn't even sure what he looked like! Akasma, like Betta, had been expert at collecting information, listening to the gossip of the cooks and the washerwomen and the stable grooms, picking up shards of information and deftly putting them all together. Even if she hadn't yet learned French, she was highly intelligent and would have picked it up quickly, and she would have found ways to gather what I needed to know. My ordinary maidservants could accomplish all the ordinary tasks— dressing me, arranging my hair, fastening my jewels—but they were not confidantes. Without Akasma I tried to calm myself by kneeling often in the private chapel of the palace. But my restless mind would not focus on my prayers, darting back and forth between Ippolito and Henri, Henri and Ippolito.

Finally the day came for me to make my official entry into Marseilles. Gowned in gold and silver tissue, the cloth chosen for me by the Duchess of Mantua because it reflected both the sun and the moon, I was mounted on a large bay gelding.

I held my head erect and smiled graciously and waved until I thought my arm would fall off. I understood well the importance of making a good impression on the crowds jamming the streets for a look at the Italian girl who had come to marry their prince. I'd have to work hard to win their affection. Although my mother was French, members of the court as well as the people in the street would not forget that I was a foreigner and not of royal blood. But I did have one undeniable fact in my favor: I was the niece of two popes. Probably for this reason the crowds cheered politely as I rode by.

I managed to do all the occasion required: Kiss the pope's ring; curtsy deeply to the king; accept his kiss; steal a glance at the nervous boy who, nudged by his father, stepped forward to kiss me as well. I looked for some sign that the young Duke of Orléans found me appealing, that I pleased him. But there was no such sign. It was as though his thoughts were elsewhere and he didn't see me at all.

We moved to the banquet hall. I could not have said what dishes were served, except that there was an endless parade of them, each presented with a flourish of trumpets. I dutifully tasted a bite here and there. I had no appetite.

Afterward, my ladies complained that the fare was quite different from what we were used to. "What barbarians the French are!" Giulietta complained. "No one uses forks. Do they even have them here?"

DURING FOUR DAYS of feasting and dancing and entertainments, I had an opportunity to observe my bridegroom. Henri was the same age I was, fourteen. He was tall and well built, his hair dark and straight, his features regular—maybe not handsome, most would say, but certainly not displeasing. He spoke hardly at all—not to his father, to his brothers, to anyone. I saw him glancing uneasily around the huge banquet hall, but his eyes never came to rest on me. I remembered stories Aunt Clarissa had told me of my parents, who had been introduced at the christening of Henri's older brother. *The very first time they met, Madeleine fell madly in love with Lorenzo, and he with her,* Clarissa often said. Watching Henri now, I knew without a doubt that this would not happen to us. Henri would never look at me the way Ippolito once did, never lift my hand to his lips, never call me "my dearest Duchessina." A bleakness settled over me.

Four days of celebration, and we still weren't married. The wedding night still loomed ahead of me. I dreaded it.

On the day before the wedding was to take place, King François and Pope Clement signed the final marriage contract, and Henri and I met formally for the first time. We were led into a vast hall, where we were blessed by the French cardinal who'd once sat next to me at Clement's dinner. In front of a huge crowd, Henri stepped forward and kissed me first on one cheek, then the other. His cold lips barely grazed my skin. He smelled of horses and wine.

The kiss prompted another of those deafening trumpet fanfares. A group of musicians struck up a stately piece, and everyone began to dance. Everyone, that is, but

Henri and me. *Perhaps,* I thought, *we won't dance until after we're married.* I wasn't sure. We sat down and watched, side by side, without exchanging a single word. Henri stared morosely into space. Occasionally his glance came to rest on a beautiful older woman strikingly gowned in black and white, widow's colors. She had long fingers, thick hair, a flawless complexion, a dainty mouth. She caught his eye and smiled alluringly. The color rose in his pale cheek as he returned her smile.

Who is she? I wondered. *And why doesn't he look at me?*

I had been taught by Suor Paolina in her lessons on the virtues that a well-bred lady did not initiate a conversation with a gentleman; it was up to him to make the first move. But Suor Paolina had obviously never met the likes of Henri, Duke of Orléans. I would have to break the rule.

"Henri," I began rather desperately, "we are fortunate to have such lovely weather for our wedding tomorrow, are we not?"

"Oui," said Henri, when he realized that I had spoken. "Quite fortunate."

I endured another dense silence. "The French style of dancing is greatly to be admired," I said. "Very graceful."

Henri sighed. *"Oui,"* he said, drawn unwillingly back from wherever his thoughts had taken him. "Quite graceful."

The silence resumed. As the dancers passed by, I managed to smile and nod and to give the impression that I was enjoying myself, which I was not—especially when I

observed Ippolito dancing with a succession of young
ladies and clearly having a fine time of it.

The beautiful woman in black and white disappeared,
and Henri's interest in the ball seemed to vanish with her.
The one thing that pulled my bridegroom from his torpor
were the antics of the court dwarf, who performed acro-
batic feats mimicking the dancers. That made him laugh
out loud. I tried to appear amused.

Will this never end?

At last it did. Henri's suite of gentlemen and my ladies
gathered to escort us back to our separate lodgings. "Good
night, *mademoiselle*," Henri said with a bow.

Doesn't he remember my name? I dropped him a graceful
curtsy. "Good night, my lord," I said, smiling, always smiling, although I was ready to weep.

Oh, Akasma, I thought as I lay sleepless in the huge bed,
if only you were here to tell me what to do!

ON MY WEDDING DAY, the morning of October twenty-
eighth, my ladies and maidservants helped me into a gown
of the palest rose-colored silk with embroidered sleeves.
They fastened over my shoulders a gold brocade robe
trimmed with velvet and precious stones and edged with
ermine. Giulietta clasped the diamond and sapphire pendant around my neck. The maidservant who'd taken
Akasma's place arranged my hair and settled on my head a

ducal crown of gold, another gift from the king. I was ready—as ready as I would ever be.

Is this how a girl should feel on her wedding day? I wondered, gazing into the mirror that my maidservants held up for me. *Neither happy nor sad but nothing at all?*

Then King François arrived to escort me to the chapel, looking exactly the way a king should, resplendent in white satin embroidered all over in gold. A cloak of cloth-of-gold covered with pearls and precious stones swirled around him.

A dozen musicians led us to the chapel, my hand resting on the arm of King François, my high-heeled chopines making me seem taller. Still, the king towered over me and had to lean down to whisper, "My dear little Catherine, you are a lovely bride."

My bridegroom waited at the chapel. I scarcely remember what Henri looked like or how he was dressed, except that he was swathed in ermine. We repeated our vows, and Henri placed a gold ring on my right hand. Pope Clement celebrated the nuptial mass. I was no longer Caterina de' Medici, *la duchessina.* I was now Catherine, Duchess of Orléans, wife of Henri, Duke of Orléans. My new husband had not yet called me by any name at all.

We next had to endure an elaborate exchange of gifts. The presentations were interminable. The pope gave François a horn, said to be from a unicorn, mounted in gold, to protect the king from poisoning. François gave the pope a Flemish tapestry depicting the Last Supper. Clement gave the king a rock-crystal box incised with twenty-four scenes from the life of Christ. François gave me three unusually large, perfect teardrop pearls. But the gift that drew gasps from all who witnessed it was a live lion, straining at the leashes held by four muscular Ethiopian servants, presented to the pope by the king.

Another banquet followed, and another masked ball at which I believe the king kissed the hand of every lady present and danced every dance, most often with one particularly lovely woman—his mistress, Anne d'Heilly, radiant in yellow silk with a circlet of emeralds in her fair hair. Once more, it was the mysterious woman, again gowned in elegant black and white, who held Henri's attention.

Then came the moment I'd been dreading: The king declared the banquet at an end, the signal for me to prepare for what was to come.

With a faint smile Queen Eleanor took me by the hand, and several high-ranking ladies of the French court led the way to the bedchamber, which had been specially prepared with herbs and perfumes for this moment. The bed itself was enormous, lavishly carved and decorated and hung with embroidered damask curtains. The ladies undressed me and placed me naked between the silk sheets, where I lay shivering with cold and fear.

Henri arrived, accompanied by his father and brothers, Pope Clement, several musicians with pipes and tabors, and a number of boisterous gentlemen who'd clearly indulged in too much wine. When the gentlemen began noisily undressing the duke, I closed my eyes until I felt Henri lie down beside me. I expected him to be as frightened as I was, but he seemed detached, disinterested.

After prayers from the pope, the company withdrew— all but King François. *Surely my father-in-law isn't going to stay!*

But apparently he was. "It is my duty to see that the marriage is consummated this night," he announced from the foot of the bed. "Touch her, Henri."

I don't remember what happened next. I did as Akasma had recommended: I willed my thoughts away from this nightmarish scene to a place of sweet-scented flowers, warm sunshine, laughter . . .

It was over quickly, and when it was, I slept.

14

Marriage

THE MORNING AFTER my wedding night the pope, the king, and members of their suites burst into the bed-chamber. They appeared delighted to find us still in bed. The pope blessed us, and then the queen's ladies arrived and draped me in a silk robe and took me away to dress me. I assume the king's courtiers did the same for Henri, although I didn't look back to see. My husband and I had not yet exchanged a half-dozen words.

During the days that followed, the celebrations continued in an endless round of banqueting, drinking, and dancing, with the antics of the dwarf for relief. King François evidently enjoyed himself enormously. Queen Eleanor smiled steadily, and Henri's sisters and brothers seemed to be having a fine time. At some point each night, when I thought I couldn't endure another minute of revelry in which I seemed to have no part, I was escorted back to the matrimonial chamber.

It was my misfortune during one of those banquets to overhear a conversation among several members of the king's court. I suppose they thought I was deaf, or that the music and laughter concealed their voices, or that I didn't know enough French to understand them. Possibly they *wanted* me to hear. In any event, their words were painfully clear.

"What can King François have been thinking?" asked one. "To marry his son to that Italian girl!"

"He was thinking of her wealth, no doubt," replied a second drily. "Certainly not of her beauty!"

The men laughed. I clenched my hands in my lap and felt my face flush.

"She's said to be among the richest women in Europe," another put in.

"But scarcely a drop of royal blood runs in her veins! I would rather have both my knees broken than bend them to that Italian merchant's daughter," the first rejoined haughtily.

Must I really sit here and listen to this? I thought miserably. I wanted to leave, to sweep by them and speak to them in excellent French, letting them know that I had understood them perfectly and would not forget their cruel words. But at that moment the ladies arrived to escort me back to the royal bedchamber. Numbly, I followed them.

Henri did not return that night—or any of the nights after—to the bed I'd expected to share with him. I didn't know whether to feel relief or disappointment. Mostly I was puzzled. *Maybe he feels the same as those courtiers,* I thought, *that he's married far beneath him to an Italian merchant's daughter with no royal blood in her veins.* Before that moment, it had never occurred to me that I was inferior to anyone.

After two weeks, King François and his court bid an elaborate farewell to Pope Clement and departed for one of the royal castles, taking Henri and his brothers with him. I wasn't unhappy to see my husband leave, but I did wonder if things might change the next time I saw him and he'd had time to get used to the idea that I was his wife. In the meantime I would stay behind in Marseilles with Queen Eleanor and Henri's sisters, Madeleine and Marguerite, until the pope sailed for Rome.

Rough seas delayed Clement's departure for two more weeks, until the end of November. Before he boarded *The Servant of God,* Pope Clement took me aside for a private farewell. As I had so many times before, I knelt and kissed the Ring of the Fisherman. I was still on my knees when the Holy Father leaned close and laid a hand on my head for a blessing. "A spirited girl will always conceive children," he whispered.

Not if Henri doesn't come to my bed, I thought, but said nothing.

———

Giulietta, Niccolà, and Tomassa prepared to return to Florence with the others. They had no regrets about leaving.

"The food here is terrible," Giulietta remarked. "Maybe you can teach these people about our lasagne and ravioli. And manners, too," she sniffed.

But Niccolà had other objections. "The French are haughty. They don't really like Italians, have you noticed? I'm afraid you're going to be miserable here. If I were you, Duchessina, I'd pack up and come home to Florence with us right now. From the look of it, I'm not sure your husband will even notice that you're gone."

So they've seen how Henri ignores me. Probably everyone else has, too.

"You know I can't go back," I reminded her. "The Holy Father would surely disown me. And what would I do in Florence? Throw myself on the mercy of Alessandro? Fate has been cruel to me in the past, but I've survived, and I will survive this, too. King François favors me. I'll be able to count on him." My words were much braver than I felt. I would have given almost anything to leave with my friends, find Akasma, and stay at Le Murate. But that was impossible.

Tomassa pulled a face. "King François flirted with me," she said, blushing. "We were dancing. He was wearing a mask, but anyone could recognize who he was. And he whispered something about going to bed with him."

"You don't even understand French," Niccolà pointed out. "So how do you know what he said?"

"I don't need to know French to understand *that*!" she insisted.

"Did you accept his invitation?" I asked slyly.

"Duchessina!" Tomassa was shocked. "Of course not! How can you take this so calmly?"

"Because I must." All at once my brave words gave way to the tears I'd been holding back. "You'll write, won't you?" I pleaded.

Before the Duke of Albany's men arrived to escort my friends to their waiting ship, I gave a small silk purse filled with gold coins to each of my friends. "I have an enormous favor to ask of you: Find Akasma, my slave. She's expecting a child. Give one of the purses to Suor Margherita and ask her to help you find Akasma. Use one of these purses to buy her freedom from Alessandro, and give the other to her in secret. Tell her where I am, and beg her to come to me if she can. Will you do that for me, dear friends?"

They promised to do as I asked, although Tomassa couldn't resist saying that she thought it was a foolish idea. "You'll never see either the slave or your money," she said.

"It's worth trying," I said.

We kissed good-bye, shed more tears, and made more promises to write. Later, from an upper terrace of the palace, I watched their ship sail out of the harbor, growing smaller and smaller, until it finally disappeared.

ONLY THE LADIES of the king's household stayed on in the south of France. All the visitors had gone home, including Ippolito, who had managed to avoid me entirely and sailed back to Rome with the pope. When my presence wasn't required, I spent as much time alone as I could, reading and writing letters to friends in Rome and Florence. But as Christmas approached, the ladies prepared to join the king at Château de Fontainebleau.

The days grew shorter as we traveled northward, away from the Mediterranean coast and its sun-warmed breezes, and the air was as sharp as a knife blade. An early winter tightened its grip on the Loire Valley. Trees were swept bare, an icy mist veiled the hills, and the ground was hard beneath the horses' hooves. We rode bundled in fur-lined cloaks. When darkness fell, we stopped at châteaux belonging to the king's friends, warmed our bones and filled our stomachs, and continued on at first light. The journey lasted twelve days.

Queen Eleanor, a quiet, stolid woman, kept apart with her ladies, many of whom had moved with her from Spain some three years earlier when she married François. It must have been as hard for her as it was for me, leaving her native land to marry a man whose language she didn't speak and scarcely understood. And it surely wasn't easy for her to realize that her husband had so little regard for her and spent most of his time with Anne d'Heilly, shamelessly flaunting his mistress in front of his patient wife.

Most days I rode with Henri's two sisters and got to know them well. Madeleine de Valois was a year younger than Henri, delicately pretty and good natured. We quickly became friends. For all her apparent goodness, Madeleine was a shrewd observer and a clever gossip. I quickly began to see the French court through her eyes. Ten-year-old Marguerite, impish and hot-tempered, often protested loudly at being left out of the interesting conversations of us older girls.

As the days passed, my questions grew bolder. "Oh, you'll get to know Anne d'Heilly soon enough," said Madeleine when I asked about the beautiful lady. "Father behaves as though he's madly in love with her, but he always behaves that way with a new mistress. Father married her off to one of his courtiers and made her husband Duke d'Étampes, to please her and to placate him. She'll expect you to call her Madame d'Étampes, now that she's a duchess. The poor old duke hardly ever sees his wife, because she's always with Father."

I wanted to ask Madeleine about the woman in black and white who had so captivated Henri's attention during our wedding celebrations, but I could not quite bring myself to do it. I was determined to learn the truth about her, but for the moment I explored the subject of the king's mistress.

"Doesn't Queen Eleanor object to her presence?" I asked, although I knew well enough that men in Italy did as they pleased, just as Frenchmen did, and their wives had nothing to say about it.

Madeleine considered this. "Maybe, but it really doesn't matter, does it? Father doesn't like the queen much at all. He promised to marry her so Emperor Charles would let him out of the horrible Spanish prison. So here she is. She lives a quiet life with her ladies. Those Spanish women dress very badly," Madeleine continued. "Have you noticed? Always out of date. Sometimes the queen's gowns are encrusted with so many jewels that you can't see the fabric underneath. It's just as well—the color is sure to be something dreadful."

I wondered what Madeleine thought of my gowns and hoped I wouldn't earn her sharp-tongued criticism.

"I'd heard that Italian women also didn't have much taste in clothes," Madeleine said. "But yours are nice, Catherine. The fabrics are of excellent quality, I've noticed, and the workmanship is very fine."

"Merci," I said. "Thank you." Her comment seemed lukewarm at best, but I had to be satisfied with it.

Also during the journey to Fontainebleau I became acquainted with the king's older sister, Queen Marguerite of Navarre, who traveled with her five-year-old daughter, Jeanne. Queen Marguerite's intelligence and good humor made her an excellent companion. Little Jeanne was a happy child who chattered merrily. By the time we reached Fontainebleau, I'd begun to look more favorably on my new life and my new family.

As our large party swept through the south gate, Porte d'Orée, a thin winter sun broke through dark clouds, bathing the towers of the château in a pale golden light. The sight stunned me. Fontainebleau was far grander than anything I had imagined. It in no way resembled the rugged stone palazzos of Florence. Formal gardens, carp pools, and deep forests surrounded the château, and its grace and elegance were reflected in the calm waters of the Loire.

My two sisters-in-law rode up beside me. "Welcome to your new home, Catherine!" said Madeleine.

"We're to share the same household," Marguerite added. "And we'll have good times together, won't we?"

My heart lifting, I assured her that we would. If only Henri shared their warm feelings!

The girls showed me to a large bedchamber with high ceilings and tall windows overlooking gardens laid out in complex geometric patterns. The maidservants had unpacked the panniers delivered from Florence, although my gowns and petticoats and robes were still in the unopened *cassoni*. The silk hangings ordered by the Duchess of Mantua were in place around the matrimonial bed. A small fire burned in the ceramic stove, taking the chill off the room.

The maidservants withdrew; everyone had gone. Beyond the tall windows a light snow was falling. I watched the sky darken until a servant came to close the heavy draperies and light the candles in the wall sconces and disappeared again. After weeks of being surrounded during nearly every waking hour by members of the royal household and their servants, suddenly I was alone.

I sat down to wait, believing that someone would soon summon me. No one did. Had they all forgotten me? Tiring of this, I set out to explore some part of the vast château, wandering through long galleries lined with glowing frescoes of allegorical subjects. Servants hurried about, but I saw no one I recognized. And although I tried to be careful to remember how I had come, I soon became lost in a labyrinth of galleries and connecting chambers.

Rounding another corner, I heard the murmur of voices and caught the faint odor of cooking. I followed the tantalizing smell until I reached an enormous kitchen. A pair of boys turned a large piece of meat on a spit. Wisps of steam rose from a huge iron kettle stirred by two cooks. A baker slid pies from a long-handled peel into an oven, and his helpers kneaded dough in a great wooden trough. A few of the workers glanced at me curiously and then went on with their chores. Most ignored me.

I wondered if I should introduce myself and was rehearsing a few French phrases in my head—*Je suis Catherine, Duchesse d'Orléans*—when a clamor outside caught our attention. The door swung open wide, letting in a blast of cold air and a swirl of snow. Men in heavy boots and leather coats carried in the carcass of a deer and dropped it on the stone floor. Someone else dumped a sack of pheasants and several hares.

One of the cooks stepped forward and addressed the tallest of the men, congratulating him on taking such a large buck. I realized then that the hunter was King François.

King and cook discussed how the venison should be prepared and when it was to be served. When the king seemed about to leave, I stepped boldly out of the shadows. "Excellency!" I said in the best French I could manage. "Have you slain this fine beast in honor of your new daughter-in-law?"

King François stopped, turned, and frowned. I dropped a curtsy. Recognizing me, he laughed, then bowed and kissed my hand. "Ah, my dear little Catherine! I have indeed, for none deserves it more than you."

François invited me to dine that evening with him and his family; I accepted gratefully—otherwise I'm not sure when someone would have remembered me. I managed to find my way back to my apartment. Later, a page came to escort me to the dining room in the king's chambers. I expected that Henri would be there, too, and I waited for my husband to send me word that he had returned. But he wasn't, and he didn't. No one offered any explanation for his absence.

"And Henri?" I inquired at last. "Was the son as successful in the hunt as his father the king?"

The king glanced at me and speared another chunk of meat with his knife. "He didn't hunt with me," he said shortly.

I couldn't think what to say next. *Then where is he? When will he be here with me?*

Little Marguerite spoke up. "He's at Château d'Anet."

Madeleine shot her sister a warning glance. The king's sister frowned. I stared at my plate, unable to swallow another bite. *Château d'Anet? Who lives there?*

HENRI FINALLY APPEARED at Fontainebleau on Christmas Eve in time for Mass in the private chapel. The next day he joined in the feasting. He scarcely looked at me, barely spoke to me. He did not visit my bedchamber that night or on any of the nights that followed. On the first of January the family exchanged gifts. I'd brought with me a number of rosaries, wrought in silver or gold with precious stones and blessed by His Holiness Pope Clement. I'd spent considerable time deciding which ones should be given to each member of the royal family, finally choosing gold with sapphires for the king, silver and rubies for Queen Eleanor and Queen Marguerite, pearls for the two sisters and little Jeanne. For my husband I chose the most dramatic piece, a rosary made of ivory, each large bead carved with a biblical scene. In return I received from him a gold bracelet and—more important to me—a pretty speech of thanks.

Still he didn't come to my bedchamber. *I must not please him at all,* I thought, and I ached at my own ignorance in not knowing how. Akasma was the only person I knew who might have helped me, and I missed her more than I missed anyone.

On Twelfth Night the king and queen entertained a number of guests at a banquet. I pretended to enjoy myself, engaging the haughty French noblewoman, seated on my left, who made it plain that she was another who thought of me as "the Italian merchant's daughter." But then I was distracted by a scene that I could not ignore.

In the center of the banquet hall sat the mysterious woman always gowned in black and white. She was smiling at Henri. Henri returned her smile with one that was ten times brighter. He rushed to her side and knelt before her. I could read every expression on his face, although I couldn't hear a word he was saying. I didn't have to. I understood it all.

I turned away from the smirking noblewoman and whispered to little Marguerite, on my right, "Who's the lady talking to your brother?"

"Oh, that's Diane de Poitiers, widow of the Grand Sénéchal. She lives at Château d'Anet. Henri loves to go there," she prattled innocently. "She's old, though—nineteen years older than Henri! You should have seen the Grand Sénéchal. Everyone said he was the ugliest man in France!" Marguerite laughed merrily. "I love gossip, don't you? Everyone thinks I'm too young to understand, but I do. For instance, I know that Madame d'Étampes hates Diane. They're great rivals, because they're both vain about their beauty, but they have to pretend to get along or Father gets angry."

"I see," I murmured distractedly as Marguerite chattered, because I could see the truth written plainly on Henri's attractive young face. *It's not the château he loves,* I thought; *it's the lady.* I pressed my lips together to stop the trembling.

TWELFTH NIGHT HAD scarcely passed when the king ordered the household to move to Château de Chambord, a castle even more impressive than Fontainebleau: six immense towers, hundreds of rooms, and eighty-four staircases, including a pair that formed an intertwining double spiral.

King François was a restless man; we moved several more times during the first winter of my marriage. Every night, no matter where we were, I retired to my bedchamber to prepare for my husband to visit me. Every night, after a servant banked the fire in the stove and withdrew, leaving a single candle burning, I lay in the great matrimonial bed and watched the flickering shadows dance against the wall while I waited for Henri's knock. Night after night I waited in vain.

Whenever I sat near him at dinner or passed by him in one of the corridors of one château or another, Henri greeted me politely. He always behaved correctly toward me, but it was clear that he had no interest in me. When I tried to talk to him, he listened with half an ear, his thoughts elsewhere. I asked him questions, which he answered in as few words as possible. As hard as I tried, I could not engage him. I was prepared to open my heart to Henri, but he treated me as if I were a complete stranger. He did not desire me.

Give him time, I cautioned myself. *He's shy and withdrawn. He'll get over it.*

But I could not help noticing that he wasn't shy or withdrawn in the presence of Diane de Poitiers.

One night, as the maidservant was trimming the wick on the candle, we heard a knock. The servant and I exchanged glances, and she scurried away as the door opened and Henri entered as though someone had shoved him. "My father the king sent me," he muttered.

"Henri, I'm happy to see you," I said, "no matter if you were sent or if you've come of your own will."

Henri attended to the matter at hand quickly and without tenderness. "I trust I didn't disturb you, *madame,*" he said, and left abruptly.

Weeping will do you no good at all, I reminded myself as I lay there alone, and gave myself over to weeping anyway. My husband did not love me. He did not care for me at all. I doubt that he ever gave me even a single thought.

15

Wife and Mistress

As winter wore on and the first signs of spring appeared, Queen Marguerite and her little daughter, Jeanne, prepared to return home to Navarre, a small kingdom in the Pyrenees between France and Spain. I was sad to see them go, for the queen had been very kind to me. I attended the customary formal farewell banquets, but before her regal procession left on the long journey south, Queen Marguerite invited me to dine with her privately, with only one or two servants present.

"Well, Catherine, my dear," she began, "I shall miss you, for I've become fond of you. You're a practical young woman, as intelligent as you are sensible, and I trust that you'll know how to use the advice I'm about to give you."

She dismissed the servants and poured more wine for both of us. "First, I'm sure you understand that your best friend at court is my brother the king. Certainly you've had plenty of opportunity to perceive that François loves beauty above all else, and feminine beauty more than any other kind."

"Yes, *madame,* I have observed that," I said.

"In fact, I once heard one of his ministers say, 'Alexander the Great attended to women when there were no affairs of state to attend to; François attends to affairs of state when there are no women.'" The king's sister smiled wryly, and I suppose I appeared shocked. But I had been observing the king and his court for long enough to know that what she said was true.

"François loves to be surrounded by beautiful women—not just beauty of face and form but of brains and wit and courage. Perhaps you've already heard of '*La Petite Bande*'?"

I had not.

"These twenty-seven young women are the king's favorites. They hunt with him, dine with him, amuse him. He chooses their gowns and pays for them himself. Inclusion in *La Petite Bande* depends on the qualities I've just mentioned. I recommend it to you."

"I don't meet the basic qualification," I said flatly. "I'm quite aware of my lack of beauty."

Queen Marguerite waved away my objection. "But you

do have the bold wit and the quick intellect that appeal to the king. And I have also heard that you are an expert horsewoman. Is this so?"

"*Oui, madame.* I am very fond of riding."

"Good. Then I shall say a word or two to Madame d'Étampes. No one is admitted to *La Petite Bande* without Anne's approval." The queen summoned her servant, signaling that the meal was over. "One more thing," she said as we rose from the table. "It will be a help to you if you have a tolerance for ribald humor. My brother enjoys nothing more than a dirty joke, and the ladies of *La Petite Bande* are expected to join in the laughter. Don't let it show if you're offended."

Then she kissed me on both cheeks in the French manner and bid me *adieu.*

ONLY DAYS AFTER I had watched Queen Marguerite's departure for Navarre, Anne d'Heilly, Duchess d'Étampes, had herself announced in my apartment. I was writing letters to my friends at Le Murate, begging for news of Akasma.

"Come riding with us!" the duchess cried gaily, snatching the quill out of my hand. "The king will be there, too!"

I sent word down to the groom to equip a horse with the sidesaddle I'd brought from Florence. In minutes my maidservant had found my riding clothes, which included the short linen underbreeches Maria Salviati had given me to wear beneath my petticoat.

When I reached the stable I found the king's stallion restlessly pawing the muddy ground and a few of the court ladies already sitting sideways on their awkward saddles. They watched curiously as the groom helped me mount and I hooked my leg around the pommel.

The king arrived, greeted us all, and leaped on his horse. When he rode off, I followed closely. The other ladies—the Duchess d'Étampes among them—fell in behind us at a decorous pace. The king seemed surprised to find me at his side. He spurred his horse into a gallop; I urged mine as well. He headed for a tall, thick hedge; I kept pace with him. His horse cleared the hedge in a smooth arc. I closed my eyes and braced myself, hoping my mare would know how to take this jump. Over we went.

Hedges, fences, stone walls were no barrier at all. The wind in my face made my eyes stream with tears. We galloped at full speed toward a wide creek. The stallion took it easily, but at the last moment my mare balked. I flew out of the saddle and over her head, landing in the soft mud of the creek bank, my petticoats up around my ears.

The fall knocked me breathless. Before I could cover myself properly and scramble to my feet, the king had circled back and dismounted and now bent over me. "Catherine, my dear, are you all right?"

"I am, Your Majesty," I gasped. "Or I will be in a moment."

Gallantly the king lifted me to my feet. I saw him glancing curiously at my underbreeches, now plastered with mud. "Designed to deprive a gallant gentleman of a glimpse of heaven," I explained, smoothing my petticoats and taking a quick look at the king to see if he'd caught my little joke.

The king stared at me for a moment and then threw back his head and burst into unrestrained laughter. Hearing the hilarity, the rest of *La Petite Bande* rode up and surrounded me, asking eager questions about my sidesaddle.

"Show them what's beneath your petticoat, Catherine," ordered the king.

I felt myself blush, but I realized that this was no time to lose courage. Slowly I raised my skirt, higher and higher, revealing my lower legs until the linen underbreeches appeared. The ladies drew surprised breaths, and King François loudly proclaimed, "'Designed to deprive a gallant gentleman of a glimpse of heaven.'"

I curtsied, letting my skirts fall to their proper place, and remounted without assistance. "Shall we continue, my lord?" I asked.

The next day I was told that I was now a member of *La Petite Bande,* by order of Anne, Duchess d'Étampes. The ladies ordered their saddlers to copy the unusual Italian sidesaddle and their seamstresses to stitch them short underbreeches gathered at the knee. From then on, wherever *La Petite Bande* went, so did I. The king clearly enjoyed my company. And if there were still members of the court who would rather have their legs broken than to bend their knees to the Italian merchant's daughter, so be it— I didn't care.

THE KING AND HIS court moved from château to château, never staying in one place more than fifteen days. Up and down we went through the lovely Loire Valley, now bursting with the colors of spring. No sooner had I learned my way around one beautiful château than it was time to move to another. Most often we returned to Fontainebleau, the king's favorite.

I might have been satisfied with this life, but I was not. All the wild rides and intellectual conversation and feigned appreciation of bawdy tales didn't make up for the fact that providing an heir was my principal duty and my biggest challenge, and I had not yet conceived a child. My husband was in love with a woman old enough to be his mother and rarely came to my bed. In public Henri continued to ignore me; I simply didn't exist. Yet, in spite of his neglect and indifference, something deep inside me responded to something I sensed in Henri, and I found myself falling in love with the man I imagined him to be beneath his cold exterior. I had known only two other young men in my fifteen years: Alessandro, who was cruel and loutish and treated me badly, and Ippolito, tender and loving but beyond my reach. Henri was different from both of them in a singularly important way: He was my husband, and I wanted him to care for me. I prayed that he would someday find some small thing in me to love.

❦

ON THE TWENTY-FIFTH of September in 1534, less than a year after my marriage, Fate once again intervened and brought my world crashing down around me: Pope Clement VII was dead. My uncle had died without paying the larger part of my dowry still owed to François and without keeping his promise to secure the Italian cities he had guaranteed for the king of France. Clement's successor, Pope Paul III, had no use for the Medici and refused to honor Clement's promises. I heard that the new pope demanded that Filippo Strozzi return the Vatican jewels Clement had pledged as collateral for the loan to finance my wedding.

With Clement dead, I no longer had any political value to François, nor had I brought him the fortune he'd been promised. Worse yet, I had not become pregnant. The king had every right to send me back to Florence in disgrace, and it was rumored that nearly everyone in France believed it was exactly what he should—and would—do.

I faced another winter painfully aware of the precariousness of my position as Henri's wife. I tried to imagine ways to awaken his interest, to make myself more desirable to him. But I could think of nothing, and I had no one in whom to confide, no one whose advice I trusted.

From the time of our first meeting, I'd been bothered by the king's attitude toward Henri. François showered all his affection on Henri's older brother, the dauphin. Their younger brother, Charles, was most like his father in his easy manner and delight in dancing, feasting, and women. But Henri was generally silent and withdrawn, often dour, not at all jovial. He disliked feasting and dancing and preferred hunting, jousting, wrestling, and other rough sports. His smiles were rare, his laughter unheard of, and his conversation was always brief, unadorned, and to the point.

All of these qualities exasperated his father. "The mark of a Frenchman is to be always lively and gay," King François declared for all to hear at a festive dinner before the start of Lent, when Henri had been even more silent and withdrawn than usual. "What ails the boy?"

The king's mistress could have told him what ailed his son, for it was Anne who explained it to me when we once found ourselves separated from the others while out riding with *La Petite Bande*. "Henri surely resents his father for turning him over to Emperor Charles in order to secure his own release. And he harbors a burning hatred of the emperor, who held him hostage for four years under the most wretched conditions."

Who could blame him? Although my months shut up in a convent couldn't be compared to Henri's years in a harsh Spanish prison, I did know what it was to be cut off from all that was familiar. Perhaps it was because of this shared experience of isolation that I felt I understood Henri, although I could not seem to find a way to reach him. And even as my love for him grew—who can explain why?—he still didn't show me the slightest affection.

WITH THE COURT constantly on the move, Diane de Poitiers often traveled with us. When she didn't, Henri stayed with her at Château d'Anet for days at a time. He seemed completely devoted to her. The entire court witnessed my humiliation. Most of them scorned me. Although the ladies of *La Petite Bande* accepted me as one of them, I felt they were as likely as anyone else to laugh at me behind my back. The exception was the Duchess d'Étampes. Anne remained my ally because she despised Diane de Poitiers and would have gone to almost any length to outdo her.

Sometimes as *La Petite Bande* rode together or gathered to dine with the king, Anne entertained us with cruel comments about Diane. "Nothing but old baggage," she said disdainfully. "She must be thirty-five, if she's a day. Her bones are surely creaking by now."

Anne was eight years younger than Diane, just as beautiful, and she had the king's love. What more could she want? I could see no reason for her jealousy, but I hungered for her bitter jibes and devoured her cutting remarks. "What a cold fish Diane is! She has ice in her veins, anyone can see that, and a stone lodges where the rest of us have a heart."

Members of *La Petite Bande* speculated on Diane's beauty secrets.

"She believes that exercise is good for the complexion," observed one lady. "And she gets plenty of sleep."

"She bathes in cold water to stimulate her skin, and she doesn't paint her face, because she believes that whatever is in those substances can be harmful."

But none of that could account for the hold she had over Henri. No one seemed to know, though, if they were actually lovers. Diane had always maintained a spotless reputation, both before and after the death of the Grand Sénéchal. But even if my husband was not enjoying the delights of her body, he was obviously madly in love with her. When she chose to welcome him into her bed, I had no doubt that he would go to her without hesitation. The power was completely in her hands.

EARLY IN THE SUMMER of 1535, I received a letter from Giulietta, describing Niccolà's wedding and her own betrothal, sending news of Tomassa's decision to become a nun, and ending with an odd message: "We have found the artist about whom you inquired. The small painting was completed a year ago and has been donated to a chapel."

I reread the message twice more before it struck me that she was writing about Akasma in a sort of code: Akasma was the artist; the small painting must be the infant she had conceived by horrid Alessandro. She must have left it on the wheel at a convent.

A month or so later one of the pages at Fontainebleau came to my apartment, delivering a message and a bowl of pudding: A girl had come to the kitchen, speaking Italian mixed with a few words of French and claiming that she had once worked in the Medici kitchen in Florence. She asked to see *la duchessina*. She was refused. Then she told the cook that she knew how to make a certain kind of orange-flavored pudding that was *la duchessina*'s favorite. The cook let her try, watching carefully to be sure this was not a poison plot. The pudding had been tasted and was declared both safe and delicious.

I accepted the pudding. One spoonful and I knew. "Send her to me at once," I ordered.

***

MY REUNION WITH AKASMA was sweeter than anything I could have imagined. We talked through the rest of the day and half the night. There was much to tell. We had not seen each other for nearly two years.

"The infant?" I asked.

"By the time she was born, Alessandro had forgotten about me, and when he heard that it was a girl, he told me to get rid of her. I took her to Le Murate," she continued, "and left her on the wheel with one of the purses you sent. It was best, don't you think?"

I nodded, although I could imagine how hard it must have been for Akasma to leave her child behind. "Maybe you should have kept her with you."

"But how? I dream that someday I'll be able to get her back. But I'm so happy to be away from Florence! Alessandro and Lorenzino go drinking and whoring nearly every night, and he has taxed the citizens until they are ready to revolt against him. Plenty of Florentines have fled, and Alessandro has exiled others. He's the most hated man in all of Italy, without a doubt. Surely the one who despises him most is his poor little wife."

I remembered sweet Margaret of Austria, the emperor's daughter, who had visited Florence while I was there, and the pleasant time we had together. "They were married, then?"

"With huge celebrations, all paid for by the citizens of Florence. I can't think of anything worse than being married to Alessandro!"

Neither could I.

Among those exiled were two of my Strozzi cousins, Piero and Leone, who were now living in France. Suor Margherita had sent Akasma to Filippo, their father, and he'd helped her to reach Piero. Piero had told her about King François's frequent moves and guided her to the court.

"What luck!" she sighed. "I never thought I'd see you again."

She brought bad news, too. A number of citizens had persuaded Cardinal Ippolito to take their long list of grievances against Alessandro and deliver them in person to Emperor Charles. "But Ippolito died on the way," she said.

I covered my face with my hands. *Poor Ippolito!* "How did he die?" I whispered through my fingers when I could speak.

"Poison."

"By whose orders?"

"Alessandro's."

We were silent for a time while I mastered my feelings. Then I felt Akasma's firm hand on my shoulder. "And what of you?" she asked. "Are you hiding the king's first grandson beneath that elaborate gown?"

I grimaced and shook my head. "I haven't yet conceived."

"What? Not yet?" She folded her arms and frowned at me. "Are you doing your duty, Duchessina?"

"I am. But Henri doesn't desire me. He has a mistress, and he spends all his time with her. He visits me only occasionally, and then because the king insists. Now my greatest fear is that if I don't give Henri an heir, and soon, the king will renounce me and send me away."

Akasma began to pace around my chamber. "Oh, my dear Duchessina! We have work to do."

Shaming as it was, I submitted to Akasma and her knowledge of herbal treatments. First she mixed shep-

herd's rod with periwinkle that she'd pounded to a pow-
der, added earthworms mashed to a paste, and had me
massage the paste into my most private areas.

Next we tried the ashes of a frog, after that the testicles
of a wild boar, and then a poultice of ground stag's antlers
mixed with warm cow dung—all to no effect, except that
my husband complained of the revolting odor.

I have no idea where Akasma acquired these exotic ingredients, and I didn't question her. Akasma always had
ways of getting what she needed.

Although she'd never learned to read, Akasma had a
gift for language. Her native tongue was a mixture of Ara-
bic, Persian, and Turkish, but she had quickly learned the
Italian dialect of Tuscany and spoke it almost flawlessly.
After only a few months in France, traveling with the
French court, she could understand the conversations of
everyone she met, from courtier to cook. She consulted
with astrologers, herbalists, and apothecaries. All offered
advice and dispensed remedies, which we then tried, no
matter how repellent.

The months passed, Henri made his dutiful visits, and
I still had not become pregnant.

"I've told you that Henri doesn't desire me," I reminded Akasma timidly. "Can you find a charm or a
potion that would turn my husband's heart away from his
mistress and toward his wife?"

"I'll try," she promised. And she did, but with no better
results.

16

Henri

AKASMA HAD BEEN WITH ME for little more than a year when a tragic event changed everyone's life: the death of Henri's older brother, the nineteen-year-old dauphin. It happened this way:

The weather had been unusually warm, but the dauphin François had insisted on his usual game of tennis. Feeling hot and out of breath when he finished a game with one of his gentlemen, he called for a glass of cold water, drank it down in one draught, and collapsed. Within hours, he was dead.

Naturally, poison was immediately suspected. But who had reason to poison him, and who had the opportunity? Suspicion immediately fell on his Italian secretary, Sebastiano de Montecuculli, who had once been in the service of Emperor Charles but who had come to France as part of my retinue. It was Montecuculli who had fetched him the water. King François, crazed with grief at the loss of his heir and favorite, blamed Emperor Charles and suspected Montecuculli of being the emperor's agent.

I believed then, as I believe now, that Montecuculli was innocent, but the king ordered him tortured in a cruel device designed to mangle the legs of the suspect until pain forced him to confess. Once the confession had been wrung from him, Montecuculli was sentenced to die. A month after the dauphin had been laid to rest, I had to watch the poor man's execution. Queen Eleanor and all of the king's court were witnesses as the wretched prisoner was lashed by his arms and legs to four horses which then galloped off in four directions, pulling the victim apart. I had never heard anything like his hideous screams. Henri was beside me, his face a stony mask.

Henri was now the dauphin, next in line for the throne, and I was the dauphine. Because I would become queen when my husband ascended the throne, some in the court who disliked me were ready to believe that Montecuculli might have acted under my orders. I knew there was someone else who would benefit even more: Henri's mistress, Diane, whose prestige rose with his.

WITH HENRI DESTINED TO become the next king of France, it was now more crucial than ever for me to provide him with an heir. I worried about the problem constantly—we had been married for nearly three years—and my determination to conceive had become my obsession.

Akasma's methods got more extreme. She coaxed me to drink a glass of vile-smelling and horrible-tasting liquid that she'd tried to disguise with various herbs. I gagged and spat the evil stuff on the ground. "I can't swallow it! What *is* it?"

Finally she confessed: "The urine of a mule," she said. "But you only need to drink a glass of it once a month. Under no circumstances may you go near the mule itself. I will undertake to get its urine for you."

"I don't care—I can't do it," I wailed.

"There are other things to try," she said soothingly.

No matter how disgusting the remedies were, we tried them. Nothing worked. I was in despair. But during those months of failure, Akasma and I were distracted for a time by news from Florence: Alessandro was dead, murdered in his bed by his cousin, Lorenzino. Neither of us wasted a single moment grieving for him.

"HAVE YOU CONSIDERED that it may be your husband who's lacking?" Akasma suggested when her cures produced no results..

But Henri quickly demonstrated that he was not at fault by impregnating a young virgin during a military junket to

Italy, later boasting that he had been with the girl for only one night. The girl gave birth to a daughter and was sent off to a convent. Henri named the infant Diane de France and gave her into the care of the woman in whose honor she was named. Diane de Poitiers, who had two grown daughters from her marriage to the Grand Sénéchal, now flaunted the baby girl in her custody. This was the final blow to my pride.

Henri no longer tried to pretend that Diane was merely his "friend." He wore her colors, the black and white of widowhood that only emphasized her beauty. He took as his emblem a crescent moon that signified the mythical goddess Diana. Their monogram, the *H* and the *D* cleverly intertwined, was placed on the trappings of his horse, at the entrance to her château, and anywhere else he could think of.

Akasma tried to comfort me. "Maybe you're looking at it the wrong way," she offered. "To me, the monogram looks like two joined *C*s within the *H*."

Her explanation only infuriated me. "You can't even read!" I shouted at her, losing my temper and my patience, as I seldom did.

At my wit's end, I paced my bedchamber, wringing my hands and worrying aloud about my biggest fear: that King François would renounce me, send me away, and find Henri a new and fertile wife, all for the good of France. I could not fail in my duty to my family. I could not go back to Florence.

Then I had a desperate idea. It would be difficult to accomplish, and I wasn't even sure I could bear to go through with it, but I outlined the plan to Akasma.

"Henri has given Diane the apartment below mine at Fontainebleau," I explained. "I want you to find a workman, a person of great discretion, who will drill a small peephole above her bed, so that I can look down on it when Henri is with her and see for myself just what it is that she does to enchant him."

Akasma stared at me. "This is madness! Spying on your rival with your husband will only make you miserable."

"I'm already miserable," I said. "And I'm not at all mad. My principal duty as the wife of the dauphin is to provide him with an heir. If I fail to accomplish that, the king will likely repudiate me. Henri will accept his father's decision. I have to find a solution to my problem before François decides to act."

Akasma never stopped shaking her head, murmuring, "No, no, Duchessina! It cannot be!"

But I refused to listen. "My entire life is at stake, Akasma. So far nothing has succeeded. I must see for myself. Order the hole drilled at once."

"As you wish, *madame,*" she said stiffly. "But I can guarantee you, the only thing you will gain from this is pain." She bowed and left the bedchamber.

Efficient servant that she was, Akasma carried out my orders. The hole was drilled and concealed with a piece of wood. I paced restlessly until the sound of laughter drifted up from the chamber below, Henri's deep and yearning, Diane's light and playful. When the laughter quieted, I moved silently to the drilled hole, removed the block of wood, and peered down at the lovers.

Akasma was right: The sight was too painful to bear. Blinded by tears, I slid the block of wood into place and tried to forget what I had seen.

THAT NIGHT I SLEPT hardly at all, and by morning I had made a decision: I would throw myself on the mercy of the king. François had rarely seen me in any but the most cheerful of moods, always ready with a quick rejoinder to his wit, able to keep up with him in the hunt or in the dance. I dressed in a simple gown with only my mother's ruby cross as an ornament, and when I was sure he was alone, I went to his chambers and fell at his feet, sobbing.

"What is it, my daughter?" He lifted my chin and gazed into my face. "Why so unhappy?"

"I've heard that you may decide to repudiate me for the good of France, because I have not been able to provide my beloved husband with an heir." I glanced up at the king through wet lashes, saw the sympathy on his face, and hurried on. "And I've come to beg Your Majesty not to send me away from all that I've grown to love, but to let me stay on in your service, even if it means humbly serving the new wife to be chosen for my dearest Henri."

The king took my hand and raised me up, my face

streaked with tears, and kissed my brow. "Don't worry, *ma chère fille*—my dear little daughter," he said, close to tears himself. "It is God's will that you should be my daughter-in-law and the dauphin's wife. So be it. May it please him to grant to you and me the blessing that we desire above all else in the world."

I wept even harder at these kind words and covered his hands with kisses. When I left his chambers, I felt that for the time being my position was safe. But I also knew it couldn't last: Malicious tongues would continue to insist that the king get rid of me, arguing that I was no good to him at all.

And I had another worry: *What if the king dies before I've borne a child? Who will support me then?*

Akasma was waiting for me with one more suggestion. "Have you discussed the situation with your husband?"

"Talk to Henri? Of course not! Henri and I seldom talk, and when we do, it's about things that scarcely matter."

"It seems to me," Akasma said, "that it might help if you did. Men sometimes know more of these matters than we think they do, although they're reluctant to speak of them."

I resisted for several days. It seemed impossible! I could hardly imagine uttering the necessary words. And yet, difficult as it was, the next time Henri made a dutiful visit to my bedchamber, I followed Akasma's advice. Nearly tongue-tied, I asked if he himself had any recommendations that might help me to conceive a child. As it turned out, he did, although it was not one I wanted to hear.

"I've given a good deal of thought to the matter," he said, "and discussed it with Madame de Poitiers."

He's talked about it with her? *There is no end to my shame!*

Henri continued, "Diane has offered to send a physician she trusts. She believes he could advise you."

I hated the idea that the suggestion had come from Diane, that he had discussed my failure with her, but I couldn't refuse. The physician was summoned, and with great embarrassment I submitted to an examination. To my surprise, so did Henri. Afterward, the good doctor made certain recommendations, which we promised to follow. Henri began to appear regularly in my bedchamber. "Diane insists on it," he said, to my intense chagrin.

Nevertheless, in a matter of weeks, with a joy I had never before experienced, I could announce to Henri, to King François, to the French court, and to the world that I had conceived a child. My husband and I were both twenty-three years old, and we had been married for nearly nine years when God granted us this gift.

THE MONTHS THAT FOLLOWED this good news were generally a happy time for me. For the first time I was treated like royalty. King François ordered that my every wish should be gratified. Henri spoke to me with something like tenderness. And Akasma went to work with potions and philters to ensure that the child would be a boy.

As the time of my confinement drew near, preparations

at Fontainebleau were made for the birth. To my extreme annoyance, Diane de Poitiers put herself in charge of the delivery—everything from the bed in which I was to lie to the midwives who were to attend me and the liquids I was to drink during my labor. It was no surprise, then, to have Diane appear at my bedside with my husband when labor began. Members of the royal household and *La Petite Bande* came to offer encouragement. King François visited frequently during the hours that my pains continued, and announced his intention to be present for the actual birth. The hours passed, the pains increased. Besides the royal physician and the royal midwife and their assistants, the only two people constantly at my side were Akasma and Diane de Poitiers. Diane ordered Akasma to leave.

"Akasma stays," I gasped.

Late in the afternoon of the nineteenth of January 1544, I gave birth to a son. As I lay exhausted and the good news went out to all corners of the nation, Henri knelt by my side and took my hand in his. "My dear wife," he said, tears in his eyes, "I am most grateful." These were the sweetest words he'd ever spoken.

We named the baby François, in honor of the king.

On the tenth of February our son was christened in the chapel at Fontainebleau at a glittering ceremony that rivaled our wedding. Three hundred members of the king's guard carried torches to light the way for a bejeweled procession that included Queen Eleanor and Henri's sisters and every member of the nobility who had ever visited the château, together with cardinals and ambassadors. The king, his sister, and Henri's brother Charles stood as godparents.

"At least it's not Diane de Poitiers," Akasma whispered as I lay in my chamber, recovering. According to the physicians, I was to have only broths for two weeks, but I persuaded Akasma to slip into the kitchen to make her orange-flavored pudding. She smuggled me as much as I wanted, and my strength quickly returned.

How the world had changed! Once scorned as the Italian merchant's daughter, I was now the most celebrated woman in France. I had ensured the succession to the throne. My place was secure, but I confess that my heart was uneasy. One thing had not changed at all: I had given Henri that which he desired most, a son and heir, but Henri was still in love with Diane de Poitiers. When Diane insisted on taking over the rearing of my newborn son, Henri agreed. I could not refuse. When her cousin was appointed governor of the nursery, Henri approved. I had nothing to say about it.

KNOWING THAT FROM BIRTH onward mortal danger threatened every child, and fearing that our son might not survive to adulthood, Henri and I continued to follow the physician's advice. Within six months I was pregnant again. Our daughter, Elisabeth, was born in April of 1545.

As soon as I had recovered from the birth, Akasma

told me that she wished to return to Florence, to find her own daughter. I tried to convince her otherwise. "How can I get along without you?" I cried. But she had been my faithful servant and confidante for ten years, and in the end I could not deny her. She promised that she would return with her daughter, but we both knew that was unlikely. It was a tearful parting when she left with a diplomatic delegation traveling to Florence.

As we embraced one last time, my beautiful Akasma whispered, "You will outlast her, Duchessina. You will endure. I have no doubt of it." I knew whom she meant, of course: Diane. With a wave of her hand, Akasma was gone.

IT WAS ANOTHER great loss to me and grieved me deeply when King François, my friend and my protector for thirteen years, yielded up his soul on the thirty-first of March 1547. My husband would now ascend the throne as King Henri II, and I would become queen of France. Yet Diane de Poitiers ruled my husband's heart. He even gave her precedence over me, his wife, at public functions and had himself seated between us.

The old king's mistress, the Duchess d'Étampes, was banished from court when he died, ridding Diane of her archrival. Henri immediately reclaimed the jewels his father had given to Anne and turned them over to Diane. But nothing was ever enough for her. Diane was an aging woman now, her legendary beauty faded, but still she got what she wanted. Henri heaped on her even more riches, more property, more power. He awarded her a new title, Duchess of Valentinois, with a new coat of arms to show her higher rank. And, to my dismay, he presented her with the beautiful Château de Chenonceau, the château I loved most of all and hoped he would give to me. Then he allotted her all the money she needed to enlarge and improve both Chenonceau and Anet.

By tradition, Henri was crowned at the cathedral of Rheims. On the twenty-sixth of July 1547, well into my third pregnancy, I watched him enter wearing a tunic embroidered with the intertwined letters *H* and *D*. Akasma wasn't there to try to persuade me that the two letters were actually back-to-back *C*s in my honor! My coronation followed nearly two years later, on the tenth of June. Thirty years old, I was ordained by God to lead the people of France if the king was unable to rule. Need I say that Diane, Duchess of Valentinois, was a prominent member of the procession?

I continued to live quietly in the shadow of my husband's mistress. Every day he visited her after the midday meal to discuss state business. He was her subject and her slave. She sent him regularly to my bed at night; as a result, I bore him more children, eventually giving birth to ten infants in all, of whom seven survived. In my last pregnancy I delivered twin girls, neither of whom lived; I myself nearly died. A welcome addition to the royal nursery was a lively little Scottish queen named Mary Stuart, who had come to live with us when she was five years old and was pledged to marry our son, François.

Henri never loved me—certainly he felt no passion for me—but he did come to respect my judgment and often tried to please me. And just to be near my husband, I put up with his mistress. It was never a good bargain.

Then my life, as I knew it, came to an end. My husband, whom I had adored for many years, was mortally wounded during a joust. Henri died on the tenth of July 1559.

My first wish was to die with him. But that was not God's will.

My second desire was to help my fifteen-year-old son François rule France with his lovely wife, Mary, Queen of Scots, at his side, and to see that my other children found their rightful places in the world.

My third was to see the downfall and ultimate humiliation of Diane de Poitiers. The urge to take revenge was strong; I could have had her imprisoned, even executed—I had that power. But I remembered what I had often heard King François say: *Vengeance is the sign of a weak ruler, generosity of spirit the sign of strength.* And so I decided not to punish her as I felt she deserved.

Within days of Henri's funeral I summoned her to appear before me in the royal chambers. She came dressed in her customary black and white. Now I, too, wore widow's black. I kept her kneeling for a long time while I

studied her face. She was nearly sixty, and her beauty secrets, whatever they were, no longer kept her beautiful. I
saw in her pallor and her trembling hands that she feared
for her life, as she should have. But she asked permission
to address me, and when I granted that permission, her
voice was barely above a whisper.

"I am most heartily sorry for any wrongs that I may
have done you, Your Majesty," she said with her head
bowed, "and I most humbly beg your forgiveness."

I nearly laughed out loud. *I am most heartily sorry for any
wrongs that I may have done you.* All those years of misery she
had caused me, summed up in one sentence? I regarded
her silently for a few moments. "Madame de Valentinois,"
I began, "because of your evil influence on King Henri II,
and your alienation of his affections from his lawful wife,
you are deserving of severe punishment." Using the royal
"we," I continued, choosing my words carefully. "How-
ever, we have decided to show clemency. You are to return
to us all the jewels given to you by King Henri II, which
you understand do not belong to you but are the property
of the Crown. Furthermore, you are to return to us the
Château de Chenonceau with all its furnishings."

I paused, to let that be understood. And then I savored the moment I had waited for and desired for so
long. "Finally, *madame,* you are banished from this court
from this day forward. We no longer wish to endure the
sight of you."

Diane rose unsteadily and made a deep curtsy. "Your

Majesty is most gracious to one so undeserving," she said, and backed slowly out of the royal chamber. The pages closed the door. I leaned back and sighed.

Diane was gone.

In the end I had outlasted my rival. Just as Akasma had promised, I had endured.

Now, in spite of my grief at Henri's death, the rest of my life would begin. I would live out my destiny as Catherine, queen of France.

Historical Notes

THE SUDDEN DEATH of her husband put into Catherine's hands the power to rule her adopted country and to control her own life. Catherine was forty years old when her son, the fifteen-year-old dauphin, François, was crowned king. His wife, Mary, Queen of Scots, became the new queen of France. Catherine, then known as Queen Mother, devoted the rest of her long life to the success of her children.

A fascinating story has been told about Catherine, a devoted student of astrology since her girlhood. Soon after her husband's death, the Queen Mother summoned her astrologer and asked him to predict her future. The astrologer took her into a darkened chamber and showed her a mirror that supposedly had magical powers, explaining that each of her sons would appear, one by one, in the mirror. The number of times the image of each son circled the mirror would indicate the number of years he would reign.

The first to appear was young King François II, whose face was barely visible; the image circled just once. Next came Charles-Maximilien, who circled fourteen times, followed by Édouard-Alexandre, with fifteen turns. Other, threatening faces also appeared, including the face of the heir to the throne if Henri and Catherine's line were to die out. It was surely not the future she hoped for.

In fact, King François II reigned just sixteen months. He died in 1560 at the age of sixteen, and was succeeded by his younger brother, ten-year-old Charles-Maximilien. Catherine, proclaimed Governor of the Kingdom, ruled as his regent. King Charles IX, as he was known when he was old enough to rule in his own right, died in 1574, having been king for fourteen years. He was succeeded by his brother, Édouard-Alexandre, who ruled as Henri III for fifteen years—just as the mirror had foretold. Until the end of her life, the power behind the throne was the Queen Mother, Catherine.

BUT HISTORY HAS never been kind to Catherine de Médicis, as she was known in France.

Detractors remember her dark side, the cruel and manipulative Madame Serpent rumored to resort to black magic as well as daggers and poison to dispense with her enemies. She has been blamed for one of France's bloodiest events, the St. Bartholomew's Day Massacre, in which Catholic mobs attacked and murdered French Protestants over a period of months. Thousands died.

Nevertheless, admirers of strong, independent women regard Catherine de' Medici as a fascinating study of intelligence, strength of purpose, and dedication to her children. Perhaps her greatest fault was her blind devotion to three sons, sickly, weak, and corrupt, and her determination to keep them in power.

But it's the human side of Duchessina, the Little Duchess who became the queen of France, that captivates: the "poor little rich girl" who learned to use her cleverness and charm to make the best of a bad situation. Although her name produces involuntary shudders among those familiar with her later years, it's hard not to be enchanted by stories (no one knows the degree of accuracy) of how she brought Italian influences to the French court—everything from painting and poetry, to cuisine and eating customs, to sidesaddles and high-heeled shoes. It was Caterina/Catherine, it seems, who took French culture and made it shine.

Catherine, queen of France, died on the fifth of January 1589, at the age of sixty-nine.